SIEGE AT HIGH MEADOW

SIEGE AT HIGH MEADOW

Louis Trimble

CHIVERS
THORNDIKE

This Large Print book is published by BBC Audiobooks Ltd, Bath, England and by Thorndike Press®, Waterville, Maine, USA.

Published in 2004 in the U.K. by arrangement with Golden West Literary Agency.

Published in 2004 in the U.S. by arrangement with Golden West Literary Agency.

U.K. Hardcover ISBN 1–4056–3075–2 (Chivers Large Print)
U.K. Softcover   ISBN 1–4056–3076–0 (Camden Large Print)
U.S. Softcover   ISBN 0–7862–6829–8 (Nightingale)

The text of this Large Print edition is unabridged.
Other aspects of the book may vary from the original edition.

Set in 16 pt. New Times Roman.

Printed in Great Britain on acid-free paper.

British Library Cataloguing in Publication Data available

Library of Congress Control Number: 2004107031

I

Cordell stood in shadow beside the glassless window of the old shack and watched the rising moon brighten the trail leading across the desert to the Hells, the mountain range marking the border between Mexico and this eastern part of Arizona Territory.

Lebow spoke suddenly from behind him. 'Do you really think Lansford's going to come riding up here and let you take him, Lieutenant?'

Cordell turned in surprise. These were the first words Lebow had spoken since his capture sixteen hours ago. Until now he had just sat as if he wasn't even aware of the rope that pinned his arms to his sides.

Moonlight spattering onto the bunk where Lebow was tied showed a gleam of light in his eyes, a hint of animation in his expression. Even so, he reminded Cordell of a lump of sweating suet. His pockmarked face was putty-colored, the features loose and flabby, showing no vitality. He was a short man, narrow in the shoulders and broad like a woman at the hips. He had little physical courage, and he had put up no resistance when Cordell caught him on the trail leading up to the Hell Mountains.

'Lansford will come,' Cordell said flatly. 'He hasn't been very far behind me since I picked up your trail.'

Lebow's voice came out nervously, 'You want Lansford so bad, you can't think of nothing else. You shouldn't hate so hard, Lieutenant. You got to think clear and careful to catch a man like him. And thinking and hating don't live well together.'

Cordell said with quiet savagery, 'Keep quiet.' His eyes searched over the sprawl of desert, probing shadows cast by scattered mounds of rock. His ears picked over the night sounds, discarding those he was familiar with—Lebow's thick breathing, the faint stir of the two horses pastured behind the shack. He was seeking some hint of Lansford's approach. But there was nothing—no sound, no movement.

Eagerness to meet Lansford again rushed through Cordell with the violence of an autumn storm. At the same time, he felt the old, familiar wariness that came whenever he had to deal with Lansford. So often the man had eluded him. Even now, with only the empty silent desert in front of him, Cordell could see the sardonic smile, hear the mocking laughter.

Lebow's voice was thin, edged with hysteria. 'If you was thinking, you'd know you ought to turn me loose.'

Cordell said without looking at him, 'Turn you loose to do what? Run and hide the way you've been doing the past five months?'

2

'At least I'd be alive!' Lebow cried. 'And I won't be for long once Lansford gets hold of me.'

'You'll be safe enough,' Cordell said dryly. 'You're both going to jail.'

'What makes you think you'll get Lansford into any jail?' Lebow demanded, his voice shrill. 'I know all about you, Lieutenant. I heard your story when I was packing supplies into Fort Douglas. I know how the provost marshal's office requisitioned you from the cavalry at the end of the war and sent you after Lansford. I know you been hunting him off and on for more'n eight years now. And you never have got him into a government jail. What makes you think you can do it now?'

His voice thinned out. 'You've caught a lot of men for the provost marshal's office. They say you're the best. But you ain't caught Lansford. He beat you every time before; he'll beat you this time too. He'll get me away from you and make me tell where I hid all the gold. Then he'll kill me.'

His words broke apart, 'And you'll have my carcass to take back to your government jail. That's all you'll have, Lieutenant! My carcass!'

Cordell turned, hammering at Lebow's hysteria that drowned out all other sound. 'Why did you hide the gold? You knew what chance you'd have of keeping it. Why weren't you satisfied with a third share of a quarter of a million dollars—Lansford must have

3

promised you that much!'

'A third share!' Lebow cried. 'That was Lansford's offer, but do you think he or that man of his, Blanton, would let me have anything once they got their hands on the gold? And I don't want only a third. All my life I've taken pennies while other men took dollars. Now I've got a fortune. It's mine now!' he shrieked at Cordell. 'It's mine!'

He slumped in his bonds. The light left his eyes, the animation died out of his face. Cordell watched as he crawled back into his strange shell. It wasn't madness, Cordell thought, that made Lebow draw away from the world this way. It was more a defense against the life that had whipped him each of his forty years. It was as if by hiding this way from life, Lebow believed he could finally defeat it.

Cordell had hoped that while Lebow was willing to talk he might tell where he'd hidden the gold. Now Cordell understood that Lebow would never willingly do that, so he turned back to the window and listened to the night.

Lebow's breathing grew too gusty for Cordell to hear beyond it. He slipped outside the cabin and into shadow made by the rocky, barren hills rising back of the shack. Here Cordell hunkered down with the automatic movement of a man who has spent a fair part of his life watching and waiting.

The desert remained silent and he turned his thoughts to the theft of a quarter of a

4

million dollars worth of government gold which had led to the capture of Lebow and the best possibility of taking Lansford that had ever come his way. The bullion that had been stolen had been on its way east from California when the war ended. Taken to Fort Douglas in Tucson, it waited for further orders to move it on. But like so many things in the postwar confusion, the records on it were mislaid and it was temporarily forgotten in Washington.

Forgotten until last spring when Lansford got wind of it and devised a scheme to steal it. Actually, Cordell figured, it must have been Blanton who stumbled across the bullion. He was a former army sergeant working as a civilian at the fort. But Blanton didn't have the cunning to work out a way to steal the gold himself, just enough to bring Lansford in to organize the theft.

Lansford's plan had his usual clever simplicity. Lebow was a familiar figure at Fort Douglas. He brought in a monthly supply train and no one paid much attention to his comings and goings. Lansford simply took advantage of this.

Last November, Lebow appeared as usual with supplies, unloaded them, and drove his string of mules away—but not as usual. In their packs, he carried the gold. And, the same day, Blanton disappeared.

When Lansford's connection with the theft was discovered, Cordell was given the job of finding him, his confederates and the gold. Now, after dogged months, Cordell had managed to discover that the original plan had been for Lebow and Lansford and Blanton to rendezvous and divide the gold. But Lebow hadn't appeared at the appointed place. He and his mules had been seen briefly, heading eastward. Then he'd disappeared as though the desert had sucked him into itself the way it sucked in water.

Once he knew Lebow had cheated Lansford, Cordell reasoned that his best chance of capturing Lansford was to find Lebow and use him as bait for a trap. He had succeeded this morning, picking Lebow and his horse up on the trail, halfway between this shack and the Hell Mountains. Sure that Lansford was following him, Cordell brought Lebow to the shack and settled down to wait.

He stirred uneasily, feeling his usually strong patience begin to unravel. Lansford couldn't have been more than half a day behind. He should have been here by now. The fact that he hadn't come could mean only one thing, Lansford was laying his own trap.

The moon rose toward the top of the spring sky. Cordell shifted his position carefully, silently, and blinked to clear his eyes of the deceptiveness in the shadows he had to look at.

The soft footfalls of a cautiously ridden horse brushed Cordell's ears. He placed the

6

sounds behind and to his right, in the narrow canyon leading through the rocky hills.

He straightened up, feeling his breath check in his throat, feeling the sweat of hope on his palms. The horse came onto the flat and stopped a dozen paces to the left, leaving Cordell between it and the shack.

The rider stepped down, ground reining the horse. Cordell recognized Lansford's slender, dark arrogance. He watched the quick, light walk and thought it was like a key to Lansford's every action. It was graceful and swift and self-contained like the man who could smile as easily when he consigned a regiment of troops to death in ambush as when he stole money left him for safekeeping. Or, Cordell remembered with still violent pain, as when he shattered a woman's trust and then turned his back on her dying—the woman Cordell had loved and had pledged to marry.

The angle of the moon threw Lansford's shadow almost at Cordell's feet. In a moment he would be level with the rock itself. Cordell's hands grew damper. He wiped them on his jeans and lifted his carbine slowly and carefully. Deliberately, he kept his finger from the trigger.

There had been a time when his desire to kill Lansford was greater than his self-control. But the futile years had changed things, dulling the pain, taking the sting from the goading whip of revenge.

Now there was no thought of killing. Cordell had pledged to deliver Lansford to a government court, and in so doing he had put a checkrein on the blind hatred that had once driven him without mercy.

Lansford came into full view. The moonlight touched the lean features with cold fingers revealing the sardonic handsomeness and the sureness all as Cordell remembered them. He counted the steps that were bringing the man within striking range.

One step. Two steps. Three.

Cordell's body tingled with uneasiness. His mind whispered, *This is too easy. Lansford is being careless.*

But Lansford moved alone on the desert floor.

Cordell stepped into the moonlight. 'Hold it.'

Lansford jumped like a cat, going into the air and turning before he landed. He struck the ground to one side, his feet spread to give him balance, his gun sliding free of its holster.

Cordell took two quick strides. With savage pleasure, he chopped the barrel of his carbine across Lansford's wrist. The gun thudded to the ground. Cordell moved a half step backward and swung his left fist with all the violence he'd inherited from the long, empty years. The blow caught Lansford on the side of the neck, driving him to one knee. He stayed that way momentarily, his empty hands

8

splayed in the dust, his head hanging. Then he rose slowly. 'Cordell, isn't it?' he murmured. 'Do you really have Lebow?'

Cordell said, 'Lebow—and now you.'

Lansford's voice was softly mocking through lingering pain. 'It's a long ride to your jail.'

II

Cordell picked up Lansford's gun and put it in his belt. He held his carbine with his finger on the trigger now, not watching Lansford but wary for any movement out in the desert. Lansford had let himself be caught too easily—as if it was what he wanted. Cordell thought about Blanton and doubled his wariness as he said, 'Into the shack.'

Lansford staggered at first as he walked ahead of Cordell. But his stride was firm and easy again by the time they entered the cabin. Cordell pushed the door shut with a swing of his heavy shoulders and lighted a lamp.

'Empty your pockets,' he ordered.

Lansford's eyes drifted over Cordell, over the solid, compact body, the long face with the slightly bent nose, the steady, implacable gray eyes. Lansford's expression showed no surprise at Cordell's dusty trail rider clothes, at his tied down holster.

'You don't look much like a government man,' he said dryly as he emptied his pockets.

Cordell watched as Lansford placed a knife, a few Mexican coins, a handkerchief, and a thin leather wallet on the seat of a broken-backed chair.

'I don't carry a hide-out gun, if that's worrying you,' Lansford said in his easy voice.

Cordell ignored him and picked up the wallet. It contained only a thin sheaf of gold embossed calling cards, each bearing the name, *Captain Montgomery Lansford.*

Cordell tossed the wallet to the chair seat. 'Which army are you a captain in this year?'

Lansford smiled. 'Whichever suits me best at the moment. There are still places in this country where it's profitable to have been in the Confederate Army.'

Cordell stared at him. After eight years he still found it difficult to understand Lansford. The man spent the war years selling secrets to both sides when he wasn't selling out both sides. When he ran out that string he'd gone around the west organizing Copperhead groups—one in Lane County, Oregon, another in northern California—and raising money he claimed would go to the South. Each time he'd disappeared as soon as his pockets were full.

Lansford replaced his possessions in his pockets. 'You're wondering why no one has killed me,' he murmured. His eyes mocked Cordell. 'You could have tonight. Why didn't you?'

Cordell picked up a length of rope and motioned Lansford to the broken-backed chair. 'I want you in prison,' he said flatly.

Lansford sat down. He had cast only a casual glance at Lebow so far. And Lebow ignored him completely. Lansford made no resistance as Cordell lashed his wrists together, took a turn of the rope around his waist and let the free end dangle.

Cordell went to Lebow and untied him. Then he led both men out of the cabin and to their horses. After they'd mounted, he roped them into their saddles. Once on his own buckskin, he took the reins of the other two horses, and started along the edge of the desert toward the trail to Tucson.

A rabbit moved on the desert floor. Cordell glanced sharply to his left. He was tired from his vigil and from reaction to the realization that his years of work might be nearing their end. The two factors combined to make him edgy and he tried to think of the hot meal and the bed waiting for him in the town of Dry Wells, a long three hour's ride to the northwest. Again he was intent on a shadow cast by a patch of rock ahead. Some of his tension evaporated when he saw the shadow held nothing more deadly than a small desert plant, its leaves folded tight against the chill of the night.

Lansford's head swung sharply around as they passed the rock. Cordell looked too, his eyes again probing the deep shadow. Then he heard a bootsole scrape sand in the opposite direction, and he knew Lansford was trying to spring his own trap.

Cordell reached for his gun. Lansford's soft, mocking laugh blended with the flat, hard crack of a rifle. A bullet burned high on

Cordell's thigh and then across the buckskin's flank. The horse lifted in sudden wild pain. Cordell swung to his right, lifting his gun, but the horse fought the bit crazily, keeping him off balance.

A deep, rich voice cried out of the night, 'Are you all right, Captain?'

'Get Cordell!' Lansford shouted.

Gunfire sounded again sending the buckskin into a twisting frenzy of fright. The reins jerked out of Cordell's hands. He reached for them and missed. His right hand clutched the saddle horn, as the horse hammered over the hard ground, seeking refuge in the rocky hills.

Lansford's final shout was thinned by distance, 'Blanton, get him! Get Cordell!' After that Cordell was too far out of range to hear anything more.

The buckskin finally stopped after it ran itself out on the twisting hill trails. Cordell slid out of the saddle to sand, fighting the pain in his leg and a desire to let himself slide into warm, beckoning blackness.

He heard sounds of pursuit—metal shoes striking rock, the faint creak of saddle leather, a voice giving a command. He forced himself to stand. He held his gun in one hand and clamped his other tight over the buckskin's nostrils. Then he glanced around and checked his position.

He was in a deep hollow, protected in front

by a tumble of rock and cut off behind by a high, sheer wall. He had searched these hills before, and he knew that there was only one way through them, a narrow gorge running from behind the old shack southwest to meet the Mexican border. And there was no way to reach that trail except by riding back to the desert, past Blanton and Lansford.

Cordell's wounded leg trembled, and he thought bleakly that he was in no condition to ride against two armed men. He had to wait here and hope he could stand long enough for Lansford to come within range of his handgun or to tire of the hunt and ride away.

Blanton's deep voice was suddenly clear just beyond a tumble of rocks. 'We haven't time to hunt him in here, Captain. I told you before, Pike Heddon and his crew were as close behind us today as we were behind Cordell.'

'Pike Heddon!' Lansford said with cold scorn. 'A fool who risks his life to rob stagecoaches and saloons, to rustle a handful of half starved cattle. He means nothing!'

'Don't underrate Heddon,' Blanton said. 'Ever since he heard Lebow hid the gold on you, he's been wanting it. Think how much he wants it, Captain. A quarter of a million dollars—a hundred times more than he ever dreamed of stealing. That kind of hunger can make even a man like him mean something.'

Small rocks made a dry cascading sound beyond the outcrop in front of Cordell.

14

Lansford's voice was closer the next time it spoke. 'I thought of the plan that got Cordell off our necks. I can handle Heddon when the time comes.'

'All right, Captain,' Blanton said. 'But we still haven't got time to waste. Not if the gold's where you figure it is. Snow can still come to them mountains this time of year.'

'The gold is there,' Lansford said with decision. 'We just have to ask Lebow exactly where.'

Blanton laughed gustily. 'Lebow isn't the cooperative kind when he don't want to be. And seems he doesn't want to be—or he wouldn't have cheated us in the first place. It won't be easy . . .'

'Lebow will cooperate,' Lansford said with cold savagery. 'When the time comes, he'll talk.'

His voice took on a note of command. 'Let's ride. Your bullet hit Cordell and his horse. If he's still alive, he won't be able to follow us far.'

Blanton's answer was lost in the jingle of harnesses and the clatter of hoofs on rock. When they were gone, Cordell dropped his hand from the buckskin's nostrils and let himself sink to the sand.

He was sure now where Lansford was taking Lebow. As he suspected when he caught Lebow this morning, the gold was hidden somewhere in the rugged, inhospitable

15

Hell Mountains.

It was a logical place for Lebow to have taken the gold. There was no habitation except for one small Mexican settlement in the single fertile valley, and there was a fair trail leading over a pass into Mexico. Cordell reasoned that Lebow had started up the pass, only to be turned back by an early winter snow. And so he had been forced to hide the gold and wait for spring thaws to clear the trails.

Cordell dragged himself up and made an effort to climb into the saddle. A sense of urgency, a need for hurry drove him now. He was not thinking of Lansford now, but of Pike Heddon.

He should have realized that vultures like Heddon and his crew of hardcases would start gathering once the secret of the gold theft got out. Unlike Lansford, Cordell had no contempt for Heddon. He was a man who combined clever, almost Indian-like strategy with vicious brutality. His great weakness was his inability to follow his own strategy if something blocked him, forced him to lose his temper.

Cordell knew that he would have little chance of success in his mission if Heddon caught up with Lansford. Then he would have only dead bodies to take back to Fort Douglas.

He finally forced himself into the saddle. He had to sit fighting the dizziness of pain for a moment. Then he rode the buckskin carefully out of the hollow and down the rocky slope.

He rode onto a ledge that gave him a view of the desert spreading toward the Hells, a day and a half of hard riding southeast. He reined in the horse and stared intently at three riders picking their way across hard ground.

Lansford was trying to hide their tracks, Cordell guessed. But that maneuver wouldn't fool an experienced tracker like Pike Heddon —or Cordell. The stretch of hard ground Lansford had evidently found lasted only a short while; then the desert floor was soft enough for even a greenhorn to read the kind of sign left by three horses.

Cordell turned the buckskin away from the ledge and headed it down to the flat. He reached the mouth of the gorge and paused. If Blanton was right and Heddon had followed Lansford, then Heddon must come this way too.

Cordell rode the buckskin into the small grassed space behind the shack, took his carbine and saddlebags, and slid to the ground. He absorbed the expected shock a little better than he'd expected, but he still had to use the carbine as a crutch to limp back to the mouth of the gorge. He stood there, listening for the sound of horses coming. But the high rock walls were silent and he turned toward the shack, satisfied for the moment.

Cordell expected to be able to hear Heddon as soon as he got within a half mile of the shack. Heddon pounded both his horses and his men.

In the cabin, Cordell built a small fire and set water to heat. He stripped off his trousers and cut away the leg of his longjohns. When the water was hot, he used some to brew coffee and the rest to wash the blood from his thigh.

The bullet wound showed as a shallow groove through the hide and into the meat of his leg. He washed the wound thoroughly, made a tight padded dressing, and laced it solidly to his leg. That done, he put on fresh underwear and worked back into his jeans. He sat down as a wave of shock struck him.

He wiped cold sweat from his face and stilled the trembling of his hands long enough to shape a cigaret and pour a mug of coffee. His saddlebags yielded a quarter full bottle of whiskey and he poured some into his coffee. The whiskey eased his pain, and when he heard the sounds he expected, he found the strength to pick up his rifle and saddlebags and limp out to the buckskin.

He pulled himself into the saddle and rode quickly to an outcropping of rock at the mouth of the gorge. He heard the thud of hoofs on rock clearly now. He looked upward to where the gorge broke over the saddle of hills. He had a glimpse of a rider silhouetted momentarily against a ridge. The man disappeared downslope. Another rider appeared briefly and dropped out of sight. More came until Cordell counted seven beside the leader.

He laid his carbine across his lap and waited, listening to the thundering of Pike Heddon and his crew fill the narrow rock walls of the gorge.

III

Fifty feet from where Cordell waited, the gorge made an elbow bend. Bright moonlight made Heddon a clean target as he swept around the elbow.

Cordell lifted his carbine and drove a shot into the rock a few feet in front of Heddon's heavy horse. It reared up and danced backward, forcing Heddon to fight the reins.

He brought it down and to a stop. He sat with his hands cupped over his saddle horn, his thick body leaning forward while he probed the darkness hiding Cordell.

Cordell called, 'Turn and ride back the way you came, Heddon. Keep out of government business.' The futility of the warning was obvious to Cordell even before Heddon's seven men rode into sight.

Heddon said questioningly, 'Cordell?'

'That's right.' Cordell felt the throb working up from his bullet-cut leg. His hands trembled and he quieted them with an effort that brought sweat springing out over his body.

'Move your men out of here!' he ordered.

'The devil with that,' Heddon yelled. 'I want Lebow.'

One man behind Heddon moved for his gun, but a quick hand signal stopped him. 'I want no trouble with you, Cordell. Give me

20

Lebow and go about your business.'

'Lebow *is* my business,' Cordell said.

Heddon straightened up. He thrust his horse forward savagely, down the steep slope of the gorge trail. Cordell fired a pair of quick shots into the rocky ground, forcing Heddon to stop a second time. Heddon cursed Cordell in a thick, wild voice. Gunfire broke out as two men well to the rear fired. The bullets struck the overhang in front of Cordell and shrieked off into the night.

Cordell called, 'The next shot is mine, Heddon. And you make the best target. I have no orders to bring you in, but I wouldn't get a court martial for showing up with your hide. Now ride out of here!'

There was no answer. Heddon sat as he had before, leaning forward, peering downslope. Cordell couldn't see his expression at that distance, but he could visualize the sullen anger on the thick, unshaven face, the gleam in the small dark eyes as hatred and frustration built up in the man.

Cordell bottled up a sigh. Even if Heddon left now, he wouldn't give up. He was a stubborn, vindictive man, a man driven by consuming greed. Cordell recalled Blanton's words: 'A quarter of a million dollars—a hundred times more than he ever dreamed of stealing before.'

The glitter of that gold would drive him to risk anything.

Heddon lifted his hand abruptly, sending his men dancing their horses back around the bend and out of sight. He followed slowly, pausing as he reached the corner of the elbow.

'I came for Lebow and I'm going to get him,' Heddon shouted down at Cordell. 'You nor nobody else is going to stop me. The next time you see me, shoot straighter. You won't get no other chance.'

He moved his horse on out of sight. Cordell sat quietly, listening as the sounds of the horses were swallowed by distance.

He guessed that Heddon would make a wide circle in order to swing around the rocky barrier and get back onto the desert flat. Once he got back to the cabin, he'd have little trouble picking up the trail that would lead him into the Hell Mountains, and to Lebow, Lansford and Blanton.

Cordell swung the buckskin toward the desert and rode cautiously to the point where the soft ground broke onto the hardpan. The sign of three horses disappeared with suspicious abruptness.

Cordell left the saddle and drove the buckskin ahead of him and away from the hardpan, back toward the shack. He moved slowly, using his hat to brush out all the tracks he could see.

Back at the cabin, he mounted again and rode slowly south, taking care to lay clear sign for Pike Heddon to read. He didn't expect such a simple trick to fool Heddon long, but right now Cordell knew he needed every hour of advantage he could squeeze out.

He not only had to capture the three men ahead of him, but he had to reach safety with them before Heddon found him and attacked.

*   *   *

Cordell's wound was bothering him. The long, hard ride across the desert had kept it sore and painful. And this second day he became aware of a fever working in him.

He looked back at the shimmering afternoon light floating over the desert. He looked ahead at the Hell Mountains, first at the barren brown foothills, then at the cool green uplands, and finally at the tall, snow-lined spires marking the summits and the boundary with Mexico.

He saw the shallow pool of water at the base of the first hills and he spent some time studying the sign men and horses had left there. It told Cordell that Lansford had gained a full half day on him.

Despite the feeling of urgency driving him, Cordell waited for the buckskin to cool down so that he could let it drink. Then he started into the hills.

The fever grew and Cordell felt himself slipping further and further away from the reality of his surroundings. Once he fell asleep

23

and awakened only when a pine branch slapped him in the face. He glanced up, startled. He sniffed the cool air.

'We made it to timber,' he said aloud. 'That little Mexican town ought to be along soon.'

The horse stepped up its slogging pace. Cordell grinned foolishly at nothing. He felt drunk. He knew he should get out of the saddle before he fell out. But his goal seemed too close now. He could make out the notch of a low pass not far ahead. With luck, he would find the town of Paradise beyond that notch.

He came through the pass and down into the valley with the evening shadows. He rode slumped in the saddle, his eyes nearly closed, his hands keeping the reins only because they were tightly looped through his fingers.

He heard a babble of Spanish voices as men surrounded the plodding buckskin. He felt hands draw him gently from the saddle and stretch him under a cottonwood. He opened his eyes wide and focused them with an effort as a tall, well-proportioned girl strode into sight. Her hair was ash blond, her eyes a bright lively green against softly tanned skin dusted lightly with freckles. She stopped by Cordell and a frown curved down the corners of her full mouth.

'This is the one,' she said in English. 'Get him inside.' She shifted to quick, fluent Spanish, '*Adentro. Prontísimo, hombres.*'

Hands lifted Cordell up. A two story adobe

building swam in front of him. A sign over the veranda announced in both English, and Spanish: PARADISE TRADING POST AND INN. M. V. ELLISON, PROP.

Cordell was carried through the dim coolness of a long barroom, down a hallway, and to a room near the rear. There was a wide, fourposter bed, made with linen sheets, and a silk-covered quilt. A stack of pillows with lace fringes were removed and a rough blanket was thrown hurriedly over the silk and linen. Cordell was laid down with infinite gentleness.

He kept his eyes open with an effort, watching the tall girl, still frowning, as she moved about the room. The door opened and a heavy-set woman bustled in. Dark eyes snapped as she looked toward the bed.

'*Ay, dios!*' she exclaimed. 'Why do you give up your room to him, Maudie?' She spoke in Spanish. Cordell gave no sign that he understood, or even that he could hear them. The girl's first words still nagged at his fever-ridden mind, bringing caution. She had said, 'This is the one,' in a tone that indicated she was expecting him.

She probably was, he thought. Lansford would have been here, and Lansford had a way with young, attractive women. Cordell could only guess at what Lansford had told her, but he knew it would be an attempt to keep Cordell from finding him.

Maudie waved the men from the room. She

25

called to the last one out, a slim boy of eighteen, '*El médico*, Pepe.'

He said, '*Si*,' and shut the door softly behind him.

Maudie turned to the other woman. She spoke in Spanish as before. 'I put him here because this is the only room with barred windows and a decent lock on the door.' She stepped to the bed and laid a hand on Cordell's forehead. Her frown deepened.

'He's burning with fever. Help me get his clothes off so the doctor can find the trouble, Mamacita.'

Mamacita began to tug at Cordell's dusty boots. 'You want to lock this man in your room, Maudie? Why do you treat a guest in such a fashion?'

Maudie unbuckled Cordell's gunbelt. 'He's not a guest. He's a man named Hart Cordell. He's the criminal Mont has been looking for.'

Mont! Cordell thought. Not Captain Montgomery Lansford to her, but Mont. The intimacy of the way she said the name struck a new note of warning in Cordell's mind. He felt the fever tighten its grip and he fought to keep his consciousness. He had to stay awake as long as possible, to hear all that this girl had to say, to know exactly what plans Lansford might have for getting rid of him.

Mamacita made a soft snorting sound and tugged at Cordell's jeans. 'Mont!' she exclaimed. 'Always it is that *Capitán* Lansford!'

26

Her voice changed, chiding a little. 'Is it good to say such things about a man to his face?' she demanded.

A flush touched Maudie's cheeks. 'He's so full of fever,' she answered, 'I don't think he knows what's going on.' Her face moved close to Cordell's. 'Where are you hurt?' she asked in Spanish.

Cordell's eyes remained open and staring. He kept his breathing at the same, slow ragged pace as before. She repeated the question in English. Still he gave no sign he heard.

'You see,' she said. She straightened up. 'And what difference would it make for a man like this to hear himself called a criminal?'

'Because the *Capitán* Lansford said he was a criminal, does not make him so,' Mamacita answered stubbornly. She loosened Cordell's belt and worked his jeans down over his hips.

'It is better that you leave now, *niña.*'

Maudie gave her a look of amused scorn. 'Who nursed that father of mine for two years after he lost a fight with a mountain cat?' she demanded. 'And who patches up your *hombres* when they nick each other with knives? I'm no child, Mamacita. I've seen men's legs before.'

Mamacita peeled Cordell down to his longjohns. She straightened up and looked intently into his face. 'I do not think this one is a criminal,' she said decisively. 'He has a good mouth. There is no meanness on it.'

'Don't be silly, Mamacita. You can't tell

27

about a man by his face.' Maudie held out her hand. 'Scissors, please.'

Mamacita brought the scissors. Maudie worked skillfully, cutting away the cloth to reveal a blood-soaked bandage.

'You need a husband, *niña*. A man to take care of.'

'I almost have a husband,' Maudie answered dryly. 'A handsome devil of a jumping bean of an almost husband.'

'There are many good men always here,' Mamacita retorted. 'Why must you wait for the bad one who seldom comes?'

'I love all the men here,' Maudie said. 'They buy my food and wine and rent my rooms and let me beat them at cards. But to marry one— no thanks. I'm too independent to make a good Mexican wife. Now, please, Mamacita, let's not argue.'

'*Gringa,*' Mamacita muttered half under her breath. 'One of our vaqueros or a man with a good face like this one is worth ten of your *Capitán* Lansford.'

'Please,' Maudie said sharply. 'I won't argue, Mamacita. You know how I feel about Mont; how I've felt ever since he first came here months ago.' She added as if forgetting she wouldn't argue, 'Besides, you know why Mont can't come here often. A government officer is always busy.'

Mamacita merely snorted.

Maudie straightened away from Cordell.

28

'That will do until the doctor comes.' She looked down. 'I want a guard on the door all the time. Mont said Cordell is very clever—and very dangerous.'

Mamaeita sounded shocked. 'You are truly going to make this one a prisoner?'

'Yes,' Maudie said flatly. 'And I'm going to keep him that way until Mont comes back and takes him to jail.'

IV

Cordell slept, woke to find the doctor dressing his wound, and slept again. When he next awoke, he knew that the fever was gone, except for a lingering feel of weakness. He lay quietly, wondering what had brought him out of heavy sleep so suddenly.

He heard a soft, rustling sound and he turned his head carefully. Maudie Ellison was crouched in front of the wardrobe. Moonlight from the barred window revealed her with clarity.

She was going through his gear, and, as Cordell watched, she drew a long white envelope from one of his saddlebags. It contained his authorization from the provost marshal's office. She opened the envelope and took out the letter with its official seal.

She held the paper to the moonlight, peering at it. Cordell threw back the covers and swung his legs to the floor. He stood up. The bed creaked sharply as his weight left the springs. Maudie gasped and scrambled to her feet.

A sharp tingle ran through Cordell's injured leg but the muscles held. He limped a step toward the girl. 'That belongs to me,' he said quietly.

Maudie said a little wildly, 'Get back to bed.

You're in no condition to be up.'

Cordell took another step. 'That doesn't give you a right to rob me,' he said with deliberate coldness.

'Rob you? I . . .' She broke off as Cordell moved closer. 'Tonio!' she cried. She went to her knees, scrambling through the gear in the wardrobe.

The door was flung open, letting light pour in from the hallway.

A young man stood there, squinting into the moon-spattered darkness, one hand at a gun on his hip. Cordell stood motionless, watching as Maudie found his gun and brought it out of the wardrobe. She got up, facing him with the gun.

Tonio said questioningly, *'Señorita?* Are you all right?'

'Help Mr. Cordell back to bed,' Maudie said coldly.

Cordell decided that this game had gone far enough. He ignored Tonio coming forward and went back to the bed. He lit the lamp on the bedside table and then deliberately slid back under the covers.

Cordell said, 'If you're looking for money, you'll find it in the other saddlebag.'

Maudie flushed. 'Go back to the hall,' she said to Tonio. He stayed where he was, looking from her to Cordell, a puzzled frown on his face. Maudie repeated her order and added, 'I can handle this now.'

Tonio stepped quietly into the hall and shut the door. Cordell said, 'You can handle what?'

Maudie looked at him steadily. 'Don't try to pretend you don't know why Tonio is guarding the door, or that you don't know why I was searching your things.'

Cordell nodded at the letter she still clutched in her left hand. 'Why should I pretend anything? That letter tells you who I am.'

Maudie glanced at the letter and flung it aside as if it had burned her. 'Mont told me what kind of tricks you'd use to get my sympathy! But I promised I'd keep you from following him. So don't waste your breath lying.'

Cordell said, 'I've known Lansford for eight years. I've spent a good deal of that time trying to put him in jail. I've also learned most of his tricks, including the one where he claims to be a government man on a secret mission. That's the story he told you, wasn't it?'

The shadow touching Maudie's eyes gave Cordell a wordless answer. He went on ruthlessly, 'He told you he was looking for a quarter of a million dollars in gold bullion that a man named Lebow stole from Fort Douglas last fall—and that I planned the theft.'

She said, 'Yes. And I believe him.'

Cordell continued to talk, telling her what had happened from the time of the theft until now. He half expected her to walk out of the room, but she listened with no movement except for an occasional deepening of the frown drawing down the corners of her mouth.

When Cordell finished, she said flatly, 'I don't believe you.'

He motioned toward the discarded letter. 'Did you read that carefully?'

'You could have forged it!' she cried.

He heard the desperation and doubt in her voice, and a wave of pity swept through him. So often Lansford made use of people like Maudie and then, when he had no further need of them, left without a backward glance.

Cordell realized that he had no time for pity. Lansford had better than a half day's lead on him now. More than that, Pike Heddon would be getting closer. The false trail Cordell had laid for him couldn't be expected to deceive Heddon long.

Cordell said wearily, 'I could have forged it, but I didn't. I'm sorry, but I told you the truth.'

She faced him with an obvious effort to keep herself under control. 'We'll see what Mont has to say when he comes back,' she said.

'He won't be back if he finds the gold,' Cordell said bluntly. 'If Pike Heddon doesn't catch him, he'll go over the pass into Mexico.'

When he had mentioned Heddon earlier Maudie had shown no sign of concern. But his repetition brought fear into her eyes—as if for the first time she understood the full meaning of this threat to Lansford.

She stared at Cordell a long moment. Then she went to her knees and threw his gear back into the wardrobe. She put the gun and the letter on top of his saddlebags and closed the wardrobe door. Her hand trembled as she turned the key in the lock.

Without looking at Cordell again, she ran from the room. Cordell lay quietly, thinking he hadn't done himself any good by his blunt attack on Maudie Ellison. Lansford would have been subtle and would have succeeded in getting what he wanted. He blew out the lamp and tried to sleep, to get back the strength fever had drained out of him. But the driving need for hurry pushed at him. Each hour he lay here meant Lansford was getting further away and Pike Heddon was coming closer.

With the first daylight, he got to his feet again and walked to the barred window. His leg moved stiffly, making his movements slow and awkward.

He studied the bars, tested them with his big hands. They were set close together and embedded deeply in the foot thick adobe window frame. There was no chance of getting out this way. He stared out bitterly at the coming day.

A barn materialized, then the timbered slopes behind it, and finally the distant peaks of the crest of mountains. Cordell stiffened as he saw a figure appear at the side of the barn.

It was Maudie Ellison, leading a saddled sorrel mare. She disappeared around the corner of the main building. A few moments later she came into sight again, riding now, with a solid looking pack behind her saddle.

Cordell swore. He swung toward the door, calling loudly, 'Tonio! *Aquí! Prontisimo!*'

The lock clicked hack and the door swung open. The sleep swollen face of the boy Pepe looked in. Cordell said rapidly in Spanish, 'The *señora*, Mamacita. Bring her quickly!'

The urgency in Cordell's voice washed the sleep from the boy's face. 'You are feeling worse, *señor*?'

Cordell said sharply, 'Bring the *señora*, now!' He took a slow step toward Pepe. The boy put a hand hesitantly to the gun on his hip, then turned and hurried out. He started down the hall, ran back and locked the door. Cordell sat on the edge of the bed, fighting impatience.

The door finally opened. Mamacita stood there, looking wide awake. 'You are hungry, *señor*?' she said in a positive voice. She came in shutting the door behind her.

Cordell shook his head. 'Did the *señorita* tell you about my letter?' he demanded in Spanish.

'*Si*,' she admitted reluctantly.

'Then you know who I am,' Cordell said.

She looked pleadingly at him. 'My Maudie has done nothing wrong, Lieutenant. I swear it. You must understand. She is in love. And when a woman loves, she must find the

35

truth about a man for herself. You must understand . . .'

Cordell said more gently, 'I'm not here to arrest her. I want to help her. Lansford is a very dangerous man. I'm not the only person looking for him. There are eight others—Pike Heddon's gang. They don't want to take him to jail—they want to kill him. If the *señorita* should be with Lansford when Hcddon finds him . . .'

He stopped as he saw hesitant half belief on Mamacita's broad face. He spoke quickly, telling her the story he had told Maudie earlier.

He added carefully, deliberately, 'I've seen women after they learned the truth about Lansford, *señora*. Some of them were badly hurt. Here.' He put a hand to his heart. He added quietly, 'One was hurt so badly that she did not want to go on living. She killed herself. That woman was to be my wife—before she met Lansford.'

It was nothing Cordell wanted to talk about, or even think about. But from the few words he'd heard Mamacita say to Maudie earlier, he judged that this would be the best way to reach the woman, to make her understand the danger Maudie was facing.

'Ah, *dios*! My poor *niña*,' Mamacita wailed.

Cordell said, 'Where did the *señorita* go just now? How does she know where to find Lansford?'

36

Mamacita hesitated again, and Cordell added urgently, 'You have to decide quickly whether to believe me or Lansford, *señora*. There is little time left. Do you think Maudie will help Lansford steal that gold when he finds it? Will she help him torture Lebow until he tells where it is hidden?'

'No, *señor*! To think such a thing is impossible!'

Cordell said, 'Lansford wants that gold, *señora*. To him it means freedom, a chance to go to a country where he will be safe from jail—and hanging. What do you think he will do if Maudie learns the truth and tries to stop him?'

Mamacita hugged herself and moaned. 'I promised her I would say nothing to you, Lieutenant. I promised I would let her learn the truth for herself.'

Cordell said, 'What good is a promise like that if her spirit is broken? Or if she's hurt—or killed—by Lansford or Pike Heddon?'

Mamacita let out a gusty breath. 'But what could I do? Maudie has ordered Tonio and Pepe to guard you. I am their mother, but they do not listen to me. They listen to Maudie.' Her dark eyes pleaded with Cordell. 'And you must not hurt them. They are only boys. They mean no wrong, Lieutenant.'

'I won't hurt them,' Cordell said. 'If you can bring me the key to the wardrobe, find a way to unlock the door, and get Pepe away for a

37

few minutes only, I can get out of the house.'

He paused and added, 'But I have to know where Maudie went, where she expects to find Lansford.'

'She went to Bowl Meadow,' Mamacita said. 'It is at the foot of the pass leading into Mexico. It is a long day's trip if one rides hard on a good horse.' She looked at Cordell's leg. 'I do not know if you could travel so far . . .'

'I have a good horse,' Cordell said.

Mamacita glanced out the window. 'Maudie has been there many times with her father. She knows the country well. She will be very difficult to follow.'

Her eyes lighted up. 'Perhaps I can talk to Pepe. And you can go with him when he takes the mules to Bowl Meadow tomorrow.'

'Mules?'

'*Si, señor.* The *Capitán* Lansford has arranged that tomorrow morning Pepe takes the mules that were left here last fall by that ugly man, the *señor* Lebow. He was in the mountains and the snow came. He returned here and left the mules to be kept until spring.'

So that was how Lansford figured out the gold was in the Hell Mountains, Cordell thought. Lansford must have tracked Lebow as far as Paradise, learned about the mules, and realized what their being here meant. And so he set himself to wooing Maudie, to have her as an ally when spring came. But he still needed Lebow to learn the exact hiding place of the gold.

Cordell said, 'Don't let Pepe take those mules up the mountain. He must stay here. Keep him away from Lansford.'

Mamacita understood. 'This *bandito*,' she murmured. 'This Pike Heddon you speak of. If he should see my Pepe with a string of mules, he would know . . .'

Cordell said, 'That's right. Now do what you can to help me, *señora*.'

'I will try,' Mamacita whispered. She turned and bustled from the room.

Cordell climbed back beneath the bed covers and tried to rest. He watched the first sunlight spread across the sky and move until it shone hazily through the window. He rose and looked out. Thin, ugly clouds were spreading out from the mountains.

'Snow,' he said aloud. 'If that thickens, it means snow.'

He went back to bed, impatient with the delay. The minutes crawled by and then, finally, the door opened again. Mamacita came in with a tray of tortillas and a cup of coffee. She set the tray in his lap. Behind her Cordell saw Pepe looking curiously and a little hungrily into the room.

She whispered, 'The key to the wardrobe is under the plate, Lieutenant. Your horse is saddled, with food in a pack. Eat quickly. I will try to keep the door unlocked and draw Pepe to the kitchen. He is a boy with a big stomach

39

and he has not eaten since yesterday.'

'*Mil gracias*,' Cordell murmured. 'A thousand thanks.'

She said softly, 'It is not for you that I do this. It is for my Maudie. She is like a daughter to me.'

Cordell wolfed down a tortilla. He said sincerely, 'I promise to do everything possible to bring her back safely, *señora*.'

He added to himself, 'If Pike Heddon doesn't find her with Lansford while I'm still trying to get out of here.'

V

Cordell finished his meal and gave the tray to Mamacita. Pepe still stood in the doorway, watching him. Cordell indicated the boy with a quick nod.

Mamacita said softly, 'My boys know how I feel about Maudie's *capitán.* They do not trust me very much.' She made a wry face. 'Their own mother—but they do as Maudie tells them!'

Cordell thought about this as he watched her carry the tray away. Pepe followed, closing and locking the door. If Tonio and Pepe suspected that their mother was helping him, his chances of getting away without a fight weren't very great. But what kind of a fight would there be? Neither boy looked particularly comfortable wearing a gun, but that didn't mean they wouldn't shoot if they were pressed.

Cordell had no desire to hurt anyone here. And although his getting away as quickly as possible was more important than Tonio or Pepe, he knew that was it simply not in him to use his gun on either one of them.

He heard soft voices outside the door. He rose and padded across the room. Mamacita was saying, 'Pepe, *niño,* you must eat. Come to the kitchen. Do you think the *señor* inside can

41

walk through solid wood?'

'I will leave when Tonio comes to watch for me,' Pepe answered stubbornly.

'Then go find Tonio and tell him to come,' Mamacita said.

Pepe was polite but firm. 'You bring him. I will wait here.'

Cordell grimaced and backtracked to the wardrobe. Mamacita's help had obviously come to its end. From here on, whatever was done, he would have to do himself.

Moving quietly, Cordell opened the wardrobe with the key Mamacita had given him. He waited for some time after the lock clocked back, but there was no sign from the hall that Pepe had heard anything. He worked more swiftly after that, putting on his clothes and gunbelt, repacking his saddlebags.

The effort of getting ready tired him more than he liked, and he returned to the bed and rested a few moments, cursing the delay. When he felt strong enough to continue, he set the saddlebags by the front wall, where they would be hidden if the door was flung open. Now he would have to use trickery. It wasn't his way of doing things and he debated some time before he decided on a plan. Finally he slipped under the uppermost blanket, pulling it up to his neck. He arranged his body carefully so that it was on the edge of the bed, his wounded leg to the inside.

Taking a deep breath, he forced a heavy

groan from his throat. He groaned again, louder, and then rolled so that he went off the bed and onto the floor with a loud thump.

Even though he landed on his good leg, he felt the shock in his wound, and he needed long seconds before he could find the strength to pull the blanket off the bed and on top of himself.

He heard the key click over. The door was flung open. Cordell lifted his head. *'Ayúdame,'* he called to Pepe peering in. 'Give me a hand. My leg . . .'

Pepe came forward, concern on his young face. He bent down to grasp Cordell's arm. Cordell said, *'Lo siento, amigo,'* and flipped the blanket up and over Pepe's head.

The boy tried to jump back. Cordell caught his ankles and pulled, bringing him down in a heap. His startled yell was muffled by the blanket, but to Cordell it sounded loud enough to bring every man in the village.

Cordell got to his feet quickly and wrapped the blanket tighter around the struggling boy. He drew his gun and pushed it hard into the writhing mass.

'Hold still,' he said coldly. 'Do as you're told and you won't get hurt.'

Pepe stopped struggling. Cordell pulled him to the wardrobe and pushed him inside. 'It won't be for long,' he said. He locked the door and tossed the key on the bed.

Pepe struggled inside the spacious wardrobe

as Cordell limped to the door and glanced down the hall. It was empty. Cordell picked up his saddlebags, drew the door shut, locked it, and put the key in his shirt pocket.

He turned left toward a door at the near end of the hall. It was unlocked. Outside, hazy sunlight struck him in the face. He blinked at it, seeking some movement toward the big barn ahead and slightly to his left. He saw no one and he limped forward.

Then he heard someone running far to his left and he tried to increase his speed. His leg protested and with an angry grunt he slowed his pace. The barren stretch of ground between the inn and the barn seemed endless, but finally he reached the blank adobe wall. He stopped to listen for the footsteps he had heard.

They had stopped. He knew the runner must have been Tonio, and that he had reached the barn first, hidden from Cordell's sight by the side wing of the inn.

Cordell sighed. If Tonio was inside, waiting for him to get the buckskin, he still might face the fight he wanted to avoid at all costs. There was nothing to do but go on—and hope.

It wasn't much of a hope, and it lasted only long enough for Cordell to round the end of the barn and start toward the big doors forming the entrance. Before he could step into the shadowed coolness inside, Tonio appeared, a gun held awkwardly in his hand.

He was panting from his hard run. 'You will stop, *señor.*' Through his gusty breathing, Cordell caught a thread of sad courtesy, as if Tonio was half apologizing for what he had to do.

Cordell stopped obligingly a few feet away. 'Mind if I set these down?' he asked, indicating the saddlebags. 'I'm getting tired.' He made a move as if to slide the saddlebags from his shoulder.

'We will return to your room,' Tonio said. 'You can carry them that distance.'

Cordell staggered a little and then went to one knee. The saddlebags slid down his arm to the ground. He put surprise into his voice. 'I guess I can't. My leg isn't as strong . . .'

Tonio hesitated, frowning. Cordell straightened up quickly, lifting the saddlebags and flinging them at Tonio's gun. He pushed himself forward with a thrust that set his wound throbbing.

Tonio swore in Spanish and tried to step back. Cordell's shoulder hit him, knocking him off balance and into the shadowy entrance to the barn. Cordell followed and they fell to the hoof-chewed dirt together.

A shaft of pain lanced along Cordell's leg as he reached for Tonio's gun. He fought a moment of blackness, and then closed his fingers over cold metal. Tonio struggled to free his arms from Cordell's greater weight. Cordell pulled the gun loose and rolled aside.

Tonio got to his knees. He looked as if he wanted to cry.

Cordell said, 'Sorry, friend, but I'm going to have to keep you quiet for awhile.'

He backed up to the wall. Taking a rope from a peg, he went back to Tonio.

'You cannot do this!' the boy cried. 'I have made the promise to Maudie . . .'

Cordell said, 'This is one promise she'll thank you for breaking. Now get over against that post and keep quiet. I haven't time to fool around.'

His movement of the gun toward Tonio was an empty threat, but he was gambling that it would be believed. Tonio looked at him sullenly and then moved to stand with his back to a thick post reaching to the roof.

Cordell turned him to face the post and built a series of loops with the rope, pinning Tonio tightly. He used Tonio's bandana for a gag, keeping it loose so that it wouldn't cut into the corners of the boy's mouth.

While he worked, Cordell explained to Tonio what he must do. 'Talk to your mother,' he said. 'She'll explain to you who I am. Think about what she says. You're a man, not a child. You know better than to do everything a girl in love tells you to do.'

Tonio made an angry sound through his gag. Cordell said, 'Lansford has gone to the mountains to find gold that the man who left the mules here hid last fall. That man and

Lansford and another stole the gold from the government. So if you let Pepe take the mules to the mountains tomorrow, he will be helping a criminal—and can be arrested himself. Do you understand?'

Tonio protested more with worry than anger now. Cordell went on, 'A man named Pike Heddon and his crew of *banditos* have been following Lansford. They'll come here— perhaps today. Tell them nothing. But do not try to stop them from going into the mountains. They are dangerous men, so don't think you or the few vaqueros here can fight them.'

Tonio made a disdainful sound. Cordell swore at him and repeated his warning. He tied the last knot and stepped back. 'You can get out of this in a couple of hours—if your mother doesn't turn you loose first. Now listen, as soon as you can, send Pepe or go yourself to Dry Wells. Tell the marshal there what I just told you. He'll contact Fort Douglas.' He flattened his voice. 'You won't be doing this for me, but for Maudie.'

He turned away and located the buckskin deep in shadow at the rear of the barn. It was saddled and had Cordell's blanket roll and pack tied on. Cordell levered himself into the saddle and sat a moment until the throbbing in his leg settled down.

He called softly, *'Hasta la vista,'* to Tonio and rode out into the hazy sunshine.

He followed the slope of a hill eastward. On its far side, he located the trail leading toward the spires that marked the crest of the mountains. He turned south and urged the buckskin to more speed.

The horse had a rough, pounding gait on an uphill pull, and Cordell felt the steady jarring working on his leg. Reluctantly he dropped the pace and rode at a walk, cursing his own weakness.

The air grew colder as the horse climbed. The thin layer of clouds thickened and dropped until the tops of the mountain peaks disappeared into them. Darkness came and Cordell pushed the horse up a long grade to a high bench he'd noticed just before sunset.

The moon was barely able to filter through the cloud cover by the time he stopped to make camp. Wearily he slid to the ground, pulled down his pack and saddle, and staked the horse in a small clearing beside a stream. He worked around the area until he found a deep, natural hollow. Here he built a fire small enough so it couldn't be seen by anyone camped above or below.

Maudie had a long start on him, but he guessed he had ridden later. And that his longer legged horse should have picked up some distance for him. Once he had eaten, he left the hollow and worked back to the trail. He saw a tall upthrust of rock just ahead and limped to it. From there he looked far down to the desert and up toward distant, higher benches.

He stared upslope for some time before he determined that the small, dancing speck he saw up there was a campfire and not just his eyes playing tricks. That would be Maudie, and he judged that she was less than three or four hours ahead of him.

He turned and looked down to the desert. There was only blackness in that direction. He was about to turn and make his way down when he saw a bright spatter of lights spring to life far down the slope.

Cordell wondered who it was—Pike Heddon or Tonio with a crew of vaqueros. Cordell reasoned that Tonio would be closer than those fires indicated if he had set up a pursuit. So it had to be Pike Heddon. And he was less than a half day's ride away now.

Cordell limped back to his camp and settled restlessly to sleep.

Tomorrow he had to ride hard, no matter what condition his wound was in. And even then he might not he able to stop Maudie before she reached Lansford at Bowl Meadow. He turned his body to find more comfort for his leg. There was no comfort for his mind. He knew that even if he managed to catch Lansford, he might be too late to get away from the implacable avalanche that was Pike Heddon and his crew.

VI

The day's ride was a hard one. The trail narrowed as it ran along the rim of a gorge and twisted its way up toward the high country. The clouds continued to thicken until the peaks were completely hidden and the notch marking the pass itself disappeared.

Cordell felt the cold and worked into his greatcoat. The wind rolled down the slopes, searching through his clothes, numbing his hands, stabbing at his wound. Then it died and the first hard pellets of snow fell. Cordell didn't know whether to be grateful or to curse the coming storm.

The trail dropped suddenly into thick forest. Here the dirt was soft and the thin snow hadn't penetrated. For the first time Cordell found sign that was easy to read. He determined that three riders and a pack animal had come this way over a day ago, and that only a short time before he arrived, a smaller horse carrying a lighter load had ridden through.

At least he had gained on Maudie, Cordell thought. Encouraged, he pushed on although it was dinner time. He ate the cold tortillas Mamacita had packed. He stopped only to water himself and the buckskin at a clear, icy spring.

He rode out of the forest to find the sky

darker and the snowfall thickening slightly. Excitement ran through Cordell as he saw dim sign of a single horse. Maudie couldn't be far ahead if the snow hadn't yet covered her tracks. He touched his heel to the buckskin's flank. 'Move along,' he said. 'Maybe we'll have company for supper after all.'

The horse neighed in soft protest. For the first time in many days Cordell had a desire to laugh. 'What are you complaining about?' he demanded. 'The lady's riding a mighty dainty piece of horseflesh. A mare, as I remember.'

The buckskin neighed again and stepped up its pace. Cordell leaned forward, ducking his head against the falling snow, his wound almost forgotten under the pressure of excitement.

Darkness came quickly and with it the wind rose again, whipping the fat snowflakes into Cordell's face. He would have missed the turn-off to Bowl Meadow if it hadn't been for the fire. He saw it to his right when he was well up the last ridge before the foot of the pass. He reined the buckskin around and tried to see through the dark and storm to judge the terrain. He hunched forward and rode for the protection of the timber he saw ahead.

He lost the fire, found it again, and lost it a second time. The last mile he rode blindly, knowing he was going downhill only because of the pitch of his saddle. Night and storm covered the country.

Then suddenly he broke into the meadow and could see the fire clearly on the far side. The wind was stronger here, driving the snow against his face, forcing him to duck deep into his greatcoat. The wound in his leg spread its ache to his hip, throbbed outward from the wound in swelling waves.

Cordell kept his eyes on the fire, using it as a guiding beacon. He held the reins tightly, fighting the buckskin's desire to turn tail to the vicious wind. He knew he should be more cautious. But the pain of his wound was too violent for him to leave the buckskin and reconnoiter on foot. He would have to risk whatever dangers lay ahead.

As he reached the edge of the firelight, a whinny came from his right. The buckskin answered. Cordell ignored its restlessness and peered through the thin screen of trees between him and the fire.

He rode to a position where he could see directly into the small camp. There was no one in sight, only the huge fire throwing a great swath of light.

'Rider coming into camp!' he called. He urged the horse forward.

The two quick shots were faint because the wind was blowing in the direction of the marksman. One bullet ticked the bark from a tree just ahead and to the right of the buckskin. The second whined close above its head. Cordell fought the reins as the tired horse reared in sudden panic. He felt the control go from the muscles of his bad leg, felt his foot slip from the stirrup.

There was the quick tilting of the saddle, the reaching for something and finding nothing. The ground rushed at him and he felt it strike the length of his game leg. Had he been shot again? Somehow it didn't seem to matter, nothing mattered but the warm darkness folding around him.

* * *

Cordell awoke to an acute awareness of heat. He lifted his head and looked dazedly around. He was lying less than a half dozen feet from the fire. It was larger than he remembered, blazing high into the snowy night and throwing great blasts of uncomfortably warm air over him.

He pushed himself to his feet and stood, swaying. His head cleared after a moment and he became aware of the heat again. He backed to a more comfortable distance from the flames. He searched the brightly lighted campsite with quick glances. There was no sign of anyone. He was alone here.

The buckskin was staked out just at the edge of the firelight. It had been stripped of saddle and bridle and was picking through the thin crusting of snow at frozen grass underneath.

Cordell turned in bewilderment. He saw his riding gear and his blanket roll under a tree a few feet away. He walked stiffly to them.

He looked down at the ground where it was still bare of snow close to the trunk of the tree. Small, neat boots had made clearcut prints in the soft dirt. Cordell had no doubt now that this had been Maudie's camp. She had been the one to shoot at him, he reasoned. And now his bewilderment was greater than ever. When he fell from the horse, she could have let him lie in the snow, leaving him to freeze to death before consciousness returned. Instead she had built up the fire and dragged him closer to it. Then she must have found his horse and staked it out where he couldn't fail to see it when he awoke.

Why? Why not just bring him around and let him do these things for himself?

The answer came quickly, numbingly. She had run again. She had not found Lansford here, but she had known where he might be, and so she had gone on.

Cordell stared out at the falling snow. It was coming down thinly now, again in small, hard pellets driven on the rising wind.

'The fool,' he whispered. 'The idiotic fool.'

He wondered how long he had lain unconscious by the fire. Long enough for the snow to have covered her tracks? He walked back toward the fire, swinging his gimpy leg stiffly. He ignored the shoots of pain that came with each jolt of his boot heel against the ground. He was looking for sign to show him which way she had ridden from the camp. At the moment, there was no room for anything else in his mind.

He found where she had brought her horse in, where it had stood while she saddled it. He hurried along the tracks until they disappeared into the trees and were swallowed by darkness. He returned to the fire and set a pitch-laden pine branch alight. With this as a torch, he continued his search. The tracks moved from the protection of the thin stand of timber and out into the meadow. Cordell shouted with relief as he saw that the wind blew the small, hard flakes out of the tracks almost as fast as they fell, leaving the hoofprints still visible.

He hurried now, saddling his horse as quickly as he could manage. He felt the ache of hunger and, once in the open meadow, the bitter bite of the mountain cold. But he had no time to waste. If the snow thickened or the wind dropped, Maudie's tracks would be blotted out in minutes.

The going was slow across the floor of the meadow. Then Cordell found a definite trail angling through a stand of timber and he made better time.

The hours and the miles folded into one another in the icy darkness. He came to a flat and paused, reluctant to subject the weary horse to more of the tormenting wind. Then he realized that there was no wind—it had died, and the snow no longer fell.

Cordell rode into the open and looked upward. There was no sign of the moon, no hint of a break in the flat, lowering sky. He felt a hint of warmth and he swore softly.

The wind had changed direction, bringing warm air up from the desert. Here in the high country that could only mean the snow would come again, but heavy and thick, a typical trail clogging, killing, spring snow.

He started to urge the buckskin across the flat and then reined in. He climbed stiffly to the ground and pulled off his gloves. He felt around until he found the tracks he sought, until he was sure they were moving due west toward a low wall of blackness ahead.

He mounted and rode on. The wall of blackness came closer and broke apart, revealing itself as a thick stand of trees. He drew close to them, looking for the trail to take up again.

There were only the trees, standing so close together that their branches interlaced. Cordell pulled the horse to an abrupt stop. He dropped to the ground and began to search for sign again. His fingers traced a pattern over the grainy snow. It had been blown into tiny ripples by the wind. Underneath the ripples it was smooth and glass-like.

He stood up, shocked by the realization that Maudie had not come this way. Somewhere back on the flat he had lost her.

He picked up the reins and started walking the way he had come. The flat seemed small when he rode across but now it was endless, a great sweep of emptiness. His leg began to throb under the steady lifting and driving. The ache from hunger grew in his belly. His movement brought sweat out on his body, and he could feel it turning cold even under his greatcoat.

At first he stopped to search for tracks every two dozen strides, then every ten strides, and finally he realized that he was on his knees more than he was on his feet. And still there were only the tracks of his own horse.

He walked on doggedly, not stopping now, thinking only of returning to the east edge of the flat, where he had first entered it and where he had first seen Maudie's tracks.

He reached the spot and almost passed it. A tree branch slapped at him, awakening him to the realization that he had entered the timber once more. He turned slowly, awkwardly and went back to the edge of the flat. He dropped to his knees and felt the ground until his fingers found the indentations he sought.

He turned westward again, stopping each few steps to drop to his knees and check for the hoofprints of Maudie's horse. The night became a mechanical stooping, rising and walking on, and stooping again.

Suddenly he became aware that the tracks

under his fingers were no longer the same. He wasn't tracing hoof-marks, but bootprints. With an effort, he fumbled inside his greatcoat until he found a match. He struck it awkwardly with numbed fingers and crouched low, holding the tiny light close to the snow.

He could see Maudie's prints clearly. They had been made after the wind died and the snow had stopped falling. He stared at them in bewilderment. There were only the boot marks; he could find no sign of the horse's prints.

He rose and retraced his steps a dozen feet. Once more he struck a match. Only the outline of bootprints glittered back at him. He went another dozen feet back and tried again. Here he read what had happened.

The snow was churned in such a way that Cordell knew Maudie had dismounted. She had led the horse a short distance. Then the tracks broke pattern, going a short ways to her left and finally returning to the straight line trail the horse had made. The hoofprints went off at a tangent also, cutting deep into the snow, telling Cordell that the horse had bolted suddenly, leaving Maudie alone and afoot.

VII

He stared around the bleak flat. The warm air stirred again, touching his bare face, his ungloved hands. He could almost taste the wetness of the coming snow.

He mounted the buckskin and reined to his left. From the saddle, he could see the chopped snow where the other horse had kicked it free in his wild run. Then he saw other tracks, angling from the far side of the flat. He did not need to stop to know what had frightened the horse. At this time of year, only a mountain lion could have sent it into such wild panic.

Cordell forced the buckskin to a faster pace. The horse's tracks were leading him to the far corner of the flat, where the timber blended into a low ridge of rock. Suddenly the buckskin sought to balk, grunting in sudden terror.

'You smell it, don't you, fellow,' Cordell murmured. He pulled his rifle from the boot and leaned forward in the saddle, his eyes searching the darkness.

The buckskin stopped, rearing. This time Cordell was prepared and he hung on grimly, fighting the reins until the horse had all four feet planted solidly again. It stood trembling, snorting in fright.

Cordell laid a hand on its neck. 'Easy,

fellow. Easy, now. Everything's under control,' he chanted softly.

He saw it now, a dark lump on the snow. Part of the lump moved and the big cat's eyes picked up the faint night light and threw it at Cordell.

'You poor hungry devil,' he said. He lifted the rifle and sighted below the eyes. The butt bucked against his shoulder with a solid feel. The rifle shot rolled across the flat to crack against the ridge of rock a short distance away.

The cat screamed. It leaped in the air, landed on its feet and charged toward Cordell. The buckskin danced nervously backward. Cordell sighted again, fired. The cat's snarl choked off as the dark mass it made against the snow stopped moving.

Cordell let out his breath. He reined the buckskin around, riding a wide circle around the dead mountain lion. The buckskin stopped again, stiff-legged, a short distance from the larger dark mass lying on the snow.

Cordell said, 'Sorry boy. It's your friend all right.' He left the saddle and walked toward the downed horse. It was a small sorrel, he saw, and it lay on its side, eyes open and glazed. Blood darkened the snow where the cat had slashed open its jugular.

'At least you died quick,' he muttered. He stepped closer and bent to the task of stripping Maudie's saddle and pack from the dead animal's back. He loaded these on the buckskin, hating to burden it so but unable to find any other solution.

He rode back the way he had come, turning westward when he found Maudie's footprints. She walked steadily, he noticed, wisely heading for the safety of the timber. He had perhaps a hundred feet to go before he reached the trees when the first fat snowflakes began sifting down.

By the time Cordell reached the trees, the snow had thickened so that his coat and the buckskin's mane were both solid white. The air continued to grow warmer and the snow fell fatter, wetter.

Cordell found a thin, twisting trail running through the trees. He started the buckskin along it and then stopped. He dropped to the ground and tested it for footprints. He found them, the small neat marks of Maudie's boots, and he rose, turning back to the horse.

It stood with front legs splayed, head hanging down. 'Beat,' Cordell said aloud. 'We're both beat, only you have sense enough to know it.'

The temptation to make camp here in the shelter of the trees touched him. He thrust it aside. Maudie was somewhere ahead, walking along in the darkness, perhaps unarmed, certainly without provisions.

Cordell tugged at the reins. 'One step at a time is all it takes, fellow,' he said. He felt the horse yield to his pulling and he started his

61

slow, gimp-legged walking again.

The trail twisted so that at first he thought it was a game trail. Then he realized it had been made by Indians. It skirted logs too carefully, followed the rise and fall of the land too faithfully to have been made by deer or any other animal.

It was gruelling footing, Cordell discovered. Only thin snow had reached down through the canopy of trees, but the floor of the trail was alive with slippery pockets of needles, with sudden upthrusts of roots, with small, hard-to see deadfalls. Twice Cordell stumbled and fell. The second time he wondered if there was any reason for rising. The pain in his leg had spread through his entire body, blotting out all other sensation.

Doggedly he climbed to his feet and went on. He felt the buckskin throw more weight against the reins as weariness dragged at its muscles. The ground sloped upward, and for a time Cordell wondered if either he or the horse could make the uphill pull. Then the trail broke into the open, following a ridge of rock and flattening out.

But here the snow had found a place to gather. Cordell was surprised at the thickness of it. Already a good two inches had fallen since he left the flat. The trail reached an upthrust of rock and made a sharp northerly angle. Cordell started to make the turn, tripped on a snow-hidden rock, and fell sprawling.

He pushed up with his arms and lifted his head. He blinked through the thickly falling snow at the upthrust of rock directly in front of him. An almost perfectly round patch of darkness lay across its face. And at the base of the patch something bulky and white moved slowly, undulating like a wounded animal dragging itself along on its belly.

*   *   *

Cordell forced himself to his feet and ran forward. He dropped to his knees. His reaching hands felt thick wool, a tangle of hair. He had found her and she was still alive. The relief welling through was chilled by a sudden thought. If he could find Maudie despite this storm, then Pike Heddon would be able to find them both easily when the storm stopped.

*   *   *

Cordell awoke to gray daylight sifting into the mouth of the shallow cave where he had dragged Maudie the night before. Smoke rose from the coals of the small fire he had kept alive through the night. He watched the smoke wander behind him, wreathe itself around Maudie's sleeping form, and then disappear slowly into the fissures at the narrow rear of the cave. Maudie's nose twitched as the smoke touched her, but she showed no sign of awakening.

Cordell rolled out of his blankets with a grunt. The cave was too low to stand in and he crawled to the fire and threw on the last of the wood he had scavenged from under the snow the night before. He found the coffee pot and carried it outside. He moved awkwardly on his knees, dragging his bad leg. It had turned stiff as a piece of cordwood while he slept.

He washed the previous night's grounds from the pot and refilled it with snow he scooped from near the cave entrance. He carried the pot back and set it over the hottest coals. Then he searched his pack and Maudie's to see what food was left. He stared in dismay at the handful of beans, the rind of bacon, the small sack of meal. Except for the coffee Mamacita had packed for him and which he hadn't used, this was their total food supply.

Cordell took his rifle and crawled from the cave. The snow was still falling in soft, thick flakes that came straight down through the quiet air. When Cordell pulled himself upright, the snow dribbled over his boot tops. He swore at it and lurched to his left, into a grove of leafless aspen where the buckskin nibbled at the few bites of twig and brown grass it could find.

Cordell saw a place farther on where the trees stood thick enough to protect the ground from the snow and he led the horse there.

Then he went on slowly, searching for deer sign. But the area seemed without life. He could hear no sounds, but the crunch of his boots, the soft hissing of the snow against tree branches, the gustiness of his own labored breathing.

Some of the stiffness began to work from his leg and he moved faster. He made a wide swing through the aspen grove and reached the trail without having seen so much as a rabbit track. Wearily, he plodded through the snow back to the cave. He knelt down and crawled inside, dragging his rifle butt-first behind him.

Maudie was crouched by the fire, boiling the beans and bacon rind and making stick bread with the last of the flour. The rich smell of freshly boiled coffee filled the smat space tantalizingly.

Cordell said, 'That's what I like. To find a woman working in the kitchen when I come in from doing the chores.'

She stared at him from tired eyes, without a sign of friendliness. 'I owe you thanks for saving me last night,' she said in a stiff voice. 'But that doesn't give you the right to expect friendship.'

Cordell slid close to the fire and pulled off his boots. He shook melting snow from them. 'And earlier, after you tried to shoot me, you helped me,' he said. 'So we owe one another nothing, and we can be strangers again. Is that what you had in mind?'

'Not strangers—enemies.' Her voice had the flat coldness of the sky outside.

Cordell went to his saddlebags and found dry stockings. He put them on and stretched his feet toward the fire. He said nothing but watched as she poured coffee and handed it to him with a piece of the hot stick bread.

He ate slowly. He was hungry, but he savored each bite as if he might never get another. When he finished, he refilled his coffee cup and rolled a cigaret.

'You never saw me until a few days ago,' he said. 'Why should you consider me an enemy? You read that letter. You know what my job is.'

Maudie's look was scathing. 'Can you deny that you came to Paradise looking for Mont—Captain Lansford?'

'No,' Cordell said.

'And you followed me here, thinking I'd lead you to him,' she continued. 'For all I know you killed my friends to get away and find Mont—so you could kill him. What else can you be but an enemy?'

'I hurt nobody,' Cordell said flatly. 'And I'm not looking for Lansford so I can kill him. My job is to take him back to Tucson to stand trial.'

Two spots of color burned on her cheeks. 'I don't believe you!'

'You mean you don't want to believe me,' Cordell told her. He rose to his knees and

66

started to pack their gear into a single pack. Maudie sat without moving, watching him.

Cordell motioned toward the beans still cooking. 'Set those off to cool if they're done,' he said. 'We'll save them for tonight.'

Maudie put the pan of beans aside. 'I'll divide them,' she said stiffly. 'I have no intention of leading you to Mont.'

Cordell continued his packing. 'The snow's over your knees out there,' he said. 'You can't afford the luxury of having an enemy right now.'

'I know these mountains,' Maudie said. 'I can find my way.'

'On foot?' Cordell asked quietly.

'I'll find my horse,' Maudie said. 'It probably joined yours during the night.'

Cordell remembered that she had been too exhausted last night to do more than fall asleep by the fire. She hadn't asked about her sorrel, and he hadn't thought it a good time to tell her.

He said now, 'He ran from you when he smelled cat. I found the sign but I was too late. I got the cat and your gear. I couldn't help the horse. I'm sorry.'

Pain crossed Maudie's features. She turned her head aside. When she looked at Cordell again, he saw that she had been crying. He said with an attempt at lightness, 'We've only got one horse between us now, and I'm not gallant enough to give you more than half of him.'

'Don't mock me!' she cried.

'I'm not mocking,' he said gently. 'I'm trying to make what happened easier for you.' He added thoughtfully, 'Pepe probably followed mc. I could try to find him for you—if that would be easier than going with me.'

She looked angrily at him. 'Why should you care how easy it is for me? I haven't a chance of getting out of here alone now. You've won. Pepe would turn back as soon as he saw the snow.'

'Nobody's won yet,' Cordell said. 'Unless it's the weather.' He finished his packing and started to crawl toward the mouth of the cave. 'Get ready,' he said. 'I'll bring up the horse.'

He crawled into the open and stood up. It seemed to him that the sky was lighter and the snow falling more thinly, but he couldn't be sure. He struggled down to the aspen grove and led the buckskin back to the mouth of the cave. He rubbed the horse as dry as he could and then put on the saddle. He shortened the stirrups and called to Maudie.

She came out of the cave, dragging the pack. Cordell helped her onto the horse and lashed the pack behind the cantle. 'We'll have to leave your saddle,' he said.

She said, 'It doesn't matter,' and looked past him into the falling snow.

Cordell gathered up the reins and started walking, breaking trail clumsily. After half a mile, he stopped and handed the reins up to

Maudie, indicating she and the horse should spell him. He dropped behind to take advantage of the buckskin's tracks.

Fighting even the broken snow gave Cordell's leg more punishment than he expected. He plodded along, his head down. He had only one thought—lifting his stiff leg and thrusting it forward. Finally he fell. He lay for a moment full length in the snow before he could find the strength to pick himself up. He lifted his head and saw that the trail was empty.

VIII

Cordell slogged on, not letting himself think that Maudie had ridden away, leaving him here without food. Without even a gun, since to relieve himself of unnecessary weight he'd hung his belt and handgun on the saddlehorn.

He rounded a bend. Maudie was walking toward him, leading the buckskin. Her eyes met his squarely. 'I fell asleep,' she said. 'I woke up and found you weren't behind us.'

She motioned back the way she'd come. 'There's a sheltered spot up ahead where we can build a fire and make some coffee.'

Cordell was too exhausted to do more than nod. Maudie swung the buckskin around and walked on up the trail. He followed slowly, not concerned now that she was getting well ahead of him.

He noticed her lead the horse off the trail and by the time he reached that place she had got a small fire going. He crawled under a natural canopy of interlocking pine branches and lowered himself wearily to the ground. He peeled off his boots and socks and put his feet close to the fire.

Neither of them spoke until they'd each drunk a cup of the coffee Maudie brewed. Then Cordell said, 'Why didn't you just ride on when you saw you were ahead of me?'

A spark of indignation flared in her eyes, then faded. 'It's your horse,' she said dryly. 'You wouldn't want me to add horse stealing to my other crimes against the government, would you—Lieutenant?'

Cordell looked curiously at her. 'Have you decided to believe I'm the man that letter claimed?'

'I don't know what to believe,' she said frankly. She poured more coffee into their cups. 'You went dangerously out of your way to help my horse—and to help me. I've been thinking about that.'

'Thinking a man bent on revenge or hungry for gold wouldn't have bothered with you?' Cordell asked.

She looked levelly at him. 'I'm not sure. You may need me to find Mont.'

Cordell shook his head. 'I've already figured out there's only one trail leading west. So I don't need your help. I didn't need it before.'

He looked out from the canopy of pine branches. The sky was no lighter than before but the falling snow had thinned out. 'And because there's only one trail coming this way, Pike Heddon won't need any help finding Lansford either.'

'You keep throwing that name at me.' Anger flared in her voice. 'Why? Is it—was it—to frighten me into believing you instead of Mont?'

The futility of fighting Maudie's belief in

71

Lansford with words held Cordell silent. Until Maudie Ellison asked freely for more of his story, he'd be wasting needed energy on useless talk.

His silence seemed to interest her more than any words he might have used. She said thoughtfully, 'Every man has a right to defend himself. When I see Mont, I'll expect him to tell me his side. But now, I'd like to hear what you have to say.'

Cordell took his time rolling a cigaret, thinking how to tell her without hurting her too much. He knew Lansford had taken advantage of her, deliberately maneuvering her to fall in love with him—a love created out of his own charm and her loneliness for someone of her own kind, someone who spoke her own language.

He said finally, hoping she would really listen, 'Just before the war ended, I enlisted. I wasn't old enough till then. My father was a civilian scout and tracker for the cavalry. He trained me for the same kind of work. I was reassigned from the cavalry to the provost marshal's office. My job was to find Lansford —and arrest him.'

'What crime did he commit?' Maudie demanded with defiant sarcasm. 'Wearing the wrong color uniform?'

'Lansford wasn't a Confederate,' Cordell replied. 'He wasn't Union either. He spent the war in a gray or a blue uniform—it just depended on which would get him the quickest profit.'

Now he kept his voice under tight control. 'He sold information to both sides. He didn't care what the results were—and a number of times men of the north and south stumbled into one of his traps—and were slaughtered like so much beef.' He paused and added flatly, 'The South wanted Lansford just as bad as the North.'

'Most of this happened before you ever joined the army,' she said accusingly. 'Yet you make it sound pretty personal—Lieutenant.'

'Later it became personal,' Cordell said in an empty voice. 'I hunted Lansford off and on for a number of years. Then I asked to be relieved of the assignment. That was later— when I knew I'd kill him if I found him.'

He threw his cigaret into the fire. 'Time washed away that feeling. So when Lansford was connected to the theft of gold at Fort Douglas and I was asked to go after him again I knew that if I found him I could control myself.'

'Control yourself,' she murmured. She stared straight at him, 'Which is more important to you now, Lieutenant—finding the gold or finding Mont?'

Cordell answered honestly, 'The government is more interested in the gold. I'm more interested in Lansford. Now let's get started. The darker it gets, the easier it is for

Pike Heddon to spot our fire.'

She remained where she was. 'It's just as I thought!' she said. 'You're really only interested in Mont, revenging yourself on him because he made a fool of you all those years.'

Cordell raked snow onto the fire. 'No,' he said, 'not because he made a fool of me. Because he betrayed the woman I was going to marry. He tricked her into loving him—the way he's tricked you. She helped him get away with money he'd stolen. When she found out what he'd done to her, she killed herself.'

'I don't believe you!' Maudie cried. 'No matter what you say about Mont, no matter how many government papers you carry, you're just what I thought you were when I first saw you—a gunman looking for someone to kill!'

Cordell rose. 'You'll believe what you want,' he said. He walked to the buckskin and led it to her. After she climbed on Cordell fixed the pack behind the cantle again, took up the reins, and started westward again.

The snow had almost stopped, he realized suddenly. He felt unaccountably chilled, and he looked up at the sky. The clouds were thinning so that here and there he could make out patches of dusky sky. He hunched down into his coat and slogged on.

When weariness began to press down on him again, he turned toward Maudie. 'How far is it now?'

She looked down at him through the quickening darkness. 'How far is what?'

Cordell said angrily, 'You weren't riding west from Bowl Meadow for exercise. You had an idea where Lansford had gone.'

'A place called High Meadow,' Maudie admitted. She pointed ahead toward an upthrust of rock a short distance up the trail. Her shoulders sagged briefly. 'If he didn't come here, I don't know where he is.'

Cordell turned and started walking again. He stopped after ten minutes of steady walking. He looked at a twisting cut that ran through the tall rocks blocking their way. The trail obviously went into the cut, but snow had drifted in, blocking it completely.

'Is there any other way through?' Cordell asked Maudie.

'There's another opening at the far side of the meadow,' she answered. 'It joins a foot trail to Paradise. But to reach that, we'd have a day's ride and another half day's walk. The country over there is too steep for horses.'

She shifted her weight in the saddle. 'I don't think these drifts are very thick,' she said. 'Most of the cut has a rock ceiling. If you'll stand aside, I'll try to push the horse through.'

Cordell stepped off the trail. He watched the buckskin as it rode forward against the chest-high snow. At first he thought this only a waste of the buckskin's strength. Then the drift gave way suddenly and Maudie and

75

the horse disappeared, into darkness.

'It's clear,' she called. 'Walk carefully. There's no light at all here.'

Cordell crawled through the broken snow until his feet touched bare rock. He could make out the bulk of Maudie and the horse ahead. He did as she told him, moving slowly, guiding himself as much by the sound of the buckskin's shoes on the rock floor as by his own sense of direction.

Suddenly there was faint night light ahead. The cut ended and Cordell moved into the still falling snow. He saw a reddish light some distance to the northwest. It flickered into brightness and then faded as a sudden gust of wind whipped snow up in a blinding cloud. The wind gentled and Cordell saw the light again.

'There's a fire ahead,' Cordell called. 'I'll take my guns now.'

Maudie was a dozen feet beyond him. She stopped the buckskin and turned in the saddle. 'No,' she answered flatly. 'I don't want any shooting.'

'You have a lot of faith in Lansford then,' Cordell said.

'Mont would no more shoot an unarmed man than I would,' she said. She lifted the reins and started the buckskin forward.

Cordell broke into a shambling, anger-driven run. His stiff leg slipped and he floundered into a snowdrift. He fought his way back to the trail the buckskin had broken and got to his feet.

He could see the buckskin now only when it moved between him and the flickering firelight. He wouldn't catch it now, but he had no choice except to go on. He'd have more chance of survival with Lansford than he'd have here in the open—with no food, no horse, and no gun.

He started in the direction of the firelight, keeping to the buckskin's trail. The wind rose again, lifting snow from the flat, open surface of the meadow and flinging it against Cordell's face. He put his head down and slogged on.

Cordell knew he'd taken the better part of half an hour to reach the protection of the trees. Relief flooded him as soon as he stepped under their sheltering branches—now he could lift his head without having his eyes beaten full of snow. But the relief died quickly as he saw how bright the firelight was now.

Maudie would have reached Lansford some time ago, Cordell thought. And that meant Lansford would be expecting him and would know he was unarmed.

Cordell looked back into the meadow. The wind had risen. Cordell noticed its direction had steadied. It was blowing straight from east to west. Already drifts were filling the tracks the horse and he had made. To buck that wind and return the way he'd come would be impossible, he knew. He could only go on and hope to surprise Lansford before Lansford surprised him.

He heard a horse neigh off to the left, and then the answering call of his buckskin. He moved in that direction, hoping his guns might still be with the horse. He went carefully, slipping from tree to tree, surveying the open spaces carefully before he stepped into them. The tree canopy overhead was fairly solid and so the snow cover on the ground was too light to hamper Cordell's movements.

He was thinking he should soon reach the buckskin, and possibly his guns, when he felt the jab of a rifle muzzle in the middle of his back. The sharp, jolt of surprise running through him made him grunt. He started to turn.

Lansford said softly, 'Don't try anything, Cordell. You don't hold the right cards this time either.'

Cordell kept on turning, holding his empty hands well away from his sides. Firelight slid through the trees and danced on Lansford's face, showing the pleased arrogance of his smile.

'Come to the fire and get warm,' he said.

IX

Cordell walked through the trees and into the camp. He looked around slowly. Lebow sat lumpishly on a high, flat rock to the right. His hands were tied together at the wrists, and a rope ran from his waist to a stunted pine growing out of a cranny in the rock overhang behind the campsite. He was back in the hole where he hid himself from the world, Cordell thought; he showed no interest in his condition but simply stared empty-eyed at nothing. Cordell turned away from him.

A large fire occupied the center of the cleared campsite. Behind it an overhang of rock thrust out above a rocky cliff face that caught the heat of the fire and reflected it. Maudie Ellison sat on the white sand floor under the overhang, both hands wrapped around a metal cup filled with steaming coffee. She didn't look up at Cordell as he stopped by the fire to warm himself.

Blanton, the former army sergeant, was crouched not far from Cordell. He had all the gear from Cordell's buckskin and he was busily pawing through the saddlebags. He lifted his bearded face with a grunt of disgust.

'Nothing but coffee and a handful of cold beans,' he said.

He swung his head toward Cordell. 'Is this

all the food you got?'

'If you don't make a smaller fire, you won't have time to eat that much,' Cordell told him. 'Pike Heddon is behind me.'

Blanton jerked upright. 'By God, Captain, did you hear that?'

Lansford was holding his gun on Cordell almost casually. He wiggled the muzzle toward Blanton. 'Tie Cordell up,' he ordered.

Maudie set down her coffee cup. 'Do you think that's wise, Mont—if that man Heddon is close?'

Lansford swung angrily on her. 'Are you on Cordell's side now?' he demanded. 'Am I supposed to let him run around loose with a gun in his hand—because he *says* Pike Heddon is on his way. That's what Cordell wants—to frighten us into letting him stay free. Can't you see that?'

Cordell noted the expression of surprise on Maudie's face. He thought, she still hasn't made her mind up all the way about Lansford. Knowing this cut away a little of the bleak emptiness that had filled him since she'd ridden away, leaving him helpless in the storm.

Cordell guessed from Maudie's earlier quietness that she had already spent some time talking to Lansford, and that she hadn't been fully satisfied by whatever story Lansford had told her. Cordell wondered if there was any chance of bringing the full truth about Lansford into the open quickly and clearly enough for Maudie to lose all doubts. Cordell needed an ally desperately. With the possibility of Pike Heddon's coming not many hours away, the situation was too urgent for hesitation.

Lansford obviously caught Maudie's shocked reaction to his anger. He said, 'I'm sorry, my dear. I keep forgetting that you don't know how clever Cordell can be.'

Cordell had a sudden desire to laugh as he realized why Lansford was being so conciliatory to Maudie. He said, 'What's the matter, Lansford, are you afraid the lady won't let you have Lebow's mules once she sees the kind of man you really are?'

Lansford took a half step toward Cordell and then stopped. 'The mules will be here when I need them.' His voice was tight, barely under control.

He was edgy, Cordell realized. Things hadn't been going according to his plans, and to a man as self-important as Lansford, that was hard to bear.

Cordell said, 'There won't be any mules until the lady goes to Paradise herself and tells Pepe to bring them.'

Maudie looked puzzled. 'Pepe was told to start with the mules yesterday morning,' she said.

'I countermanded that order,' Cordell said dryly. 'And so did Mamacita and Tonio. They have no intention of helping Lansford until they're sure you're all right.'

He looked at Lansford again, and this time he laughed aloud. 'You don't need those mules anyway,' Cordell said. 'You haven't got anything to pack away on them.'

Lansford said savagely to Blanton. 'Tie him up, I told you! Or are you so afraid of Pike Heddon that you want Cordell to protect you?'

Blanton said in his softly rumbling voice, 'I'll tie him, but don't get uppity with me, Captain. You're not my commanding officer.'

He bent down and picked up a short length of rope, motioning Cordell to go to the rear of the overhang.

Maudie said, 'Is that necessary? He isn't armed, and he's been wounded. What can he do to you?'

Cordell slid down and rested his back against warm rock. He held his wrists toward Blanton. 'I give Lansford a bad conscience—so does Lebow,' he said to Maudie.

Lansford said coldly, 'Tie his ankles too, Sergeant. I don't want him kicking us to death in the night.'

'Mont!' Maudie cried.

Lansford swung to her. 'I'm in charge here. I'll run this camp the way I see best.' He took a deep, steadying breath. 'I'm sorry. But maybe now you can see what I mean about Cordell's being clever. He hasn't been in camp ten minutes and already he has us at each other's throats.'

Cordell wanted to laugh again. He wondered at this strange lightheartedness. It was almost as if he were floating above the camp, looking down on its happenings and yet not actually part of them. The fire wavered in front of his eyes so he closed them. When he opened them, the flames danced gleefully but steadily. It was tiredness, he realized. He was too close to exhaustion to think clearly, to really be able to believe the danger threatening them all.

Maudie said nothing to Lansford. She rose and walked to the fire. There she found two cups and poured coffee in them. She carried one to Cordell, standing patiently until Blanton finished roping his ankles, then placing the cup in his bound hands. She looked at a point beyond him, not meeting his eyes.

Cordell said, 'Thanks.'

Maudie turned wordlessly away and went toward the rock where Lebow sat. Halfway to it, she stopped and looked pointedly at Lansford. 'Maybe I should have asked permission to approach the prisoners, *Captain?*'

Lansford's face flushed. 'There's no need to take that attitude. You're only playing into Cordell's hands.'

Maudie turned and walked to Lebow. Cordell watched. He noticed the strange way Lebow shrank back at her approach, spreading his unbound legs in a peculiar way and lifting his tied arms above his head.

Maudie offered him the coffee. He stared at her, his lumpish face blank. She said gently, 'Take it, please.'

He relaxed slowly, returning to his former position. A faint gleam of life touched his eyes and he took the coffee courteously.

He said, 'Thanks, ma'am,' in his thick voice and looked away.

Cordell watched the gleam fade from Lebow's eyes as Maudie walked away. He lifted his coffee cup to his mouth almost as awkwardly as Lebow. He sipped thoughtfully, an idea dancing tantalizingly on the edge of his tired mind. Before he could find energy to bring the idea into focus, Blanton spoke to him.

'Is that story about Heddon the truth, Cordell?'

Cordell saw that Lansford was listening too. He said carefully, clearly, 'Heddon was coming after Lebow the night you shot me, Blanton. I turned him back. But he wouldn't waste more than half a day going around the hills. Once he got to the desert, he'd have no trouble finding your sign or mine.'

'You're telling us what he might do, not what he did,' Lansford said. He looked at Maudie. 'I told you he was trying to frighten us with a bogey man story.'

Cordell said, 'What he might have done and what he did are the same thing. Night before last I saw his campfire down the trail from me.'

He paused and added, 'He has seven men riding with him.'

'By God!' Blanton cried.

'Don't be a fool!' Lansford said angrily. 'How do you know Cordell is telling the truth? And what difference does it make—there's no sign for anyone to follow after this snowstorm.'

'I followed sign,' Cordell said quietly.

Blanton glanced nervously at the trees, as if half expecting Pike Heddon and his crew to burst through them at any moment. 'Believe what you want, Captain, but if you use them brains of yours, you'll stay awake tonight and get out of here quick as you can tomorrow.'

X

'I didn't come all this way to turn tail and run because a bumbling fool like Pike Heddon just might be behind me,' Lansford said contemptuously.

Blanton's head swung toward Lebow. 'It's pure common sense, Captain,' he argued. 'We aren't any closer to that gold than we were down in Paradise. Let Heddon make Lebow tell where it is. Then when he's got it, we can take it away from him.'

Maudie threw a wondering look at him, and he added very hastily, 'Just because we're government men, Captain, doesn't mean Heddon wouldn't shoot us down as fast as he would someone like Cordell.'

Cordell glanced at Maudie, seeking her reaction, but the weariness that had been dogging him finally caught up. His eyes closed despite his efforts to keep them open. He was barely aware of the coffee cup slipping from his fingers. He felt the warmth of the liquid on his leg, and then nothing.

*　　　*　　　*

A sudden flaring of light brought him out of the deep, coma-like sleep of exhaustion. He blinked against the brightness. Maudie was

86

throwing wood on the fire. Lebow was still sitting like an ungainly bird on the big rock. Lansford and Blanton were nowhere in sight.

Then they appeared suddenly, coming through the trees from the direction of the meadow. Blanton stopped and stared at Maudie. He ran toward her. 'What are you trying to do, show them where we are?'

He lifted a long stick and tried to knock some of the fresh pieces from the flames.

Maudie said, 'The fire was down to coals. There wasn't enough heat to reach Mr. Lebow.'

Blanton knocked a flaming branch into the open and stomped on it with his snowcovered boots. 'Ain't that too bad! Maybe if he freezes awhile, he'll tell us where he hid the gold.'

'That's enough, Sergeant!' Lansford snapped.

Blanton whirled on him, 'You saw that firelight showing through the cut. You know what it means!'

'I saw it,' Lansford admitted. He sounded grudging.

'Heddon and his men,' Blanton cried. 'They know where we are. They'll be all over us by morning.'

Cordell said dryly, 'If Heddon already knows where we are, what difference does it make how big our fire is?'

Blanton swung toward him, big fists clenched. He stopped, grunting. Maudie was continuing the work she'd been doing before, throwing wood from a small pile onto the flames. Blanton glanced at her, but did nothing.

He said sourly, 'It doesn't make sense, trying to fight an army four times the size of yours. I say, let's get out of here.'

'And how do you plan to get out now?' Lansford asked heavily. 'Ask Heddon to let us leave the way we came?'

He strolled to the fire and examined the coffee pot. It was empty and he handed it to Maudie. 'Make some more, my dear. Apparently we won't be getting much sleep tonight.'

Blanton said to Lansford, 'I told you. This morning I found that cut through the rocks on the west side. It's got a little snow blown in it, but we can buck through with horses.'

'Buck through to where?' Cordell asked. He was wide awake now, feeling somewhat refreshed, and he watched Lansford and Blanton closely. Since their return a few moments ago, he'd sensed tension building up. For the first time Lansford seemed willing to admit aloud that he was in a dangerous situation.

Lansford glanced at Maudie who was putting the coffee pot on to heat. 'You know the country,' he said. 'Where does the west side cut lead to?'

'A foot trail down to Paradise,' she admitted.

'It's very steep. You couldn't take the horses.'

'Is that the only trail?' Lansford demanded.

'You can ride south,' Maudie said. 'But you'll only end in the Mexican desert. The Indians there aren't too friendly.'

'A foot trail's better than nothing,' Blanton said. 'Now let's pack up and get out while we still got our hides.'

Lansford stared thoughtfully toward the trees. He said suddenly to Blanton, 'How is that buckskin of Cordell's, Sergeant?'

'Strong,' Blanton said. 'But the girl told you we can't take the stock, so what difference does it make?'

Cordell stretched and looked straight into Blanton's eyes. 'All the road agents in Arizona Territory couldn't drive Lansford away without the gold,' he told him.

The smile on Lansford's face was thin. 'You're right,' he said. 'I won't leave here without the gold. I came here to get it—and I'm going to do just that.'

Maudie had a handful of coffee ready to throw into the pot. She stopped, her fist in the air, her eyes wonderingly on Lansford.

She said, 'Believe me, Mont. We can't take horses down to Paradise unless we go back through Bowl Meadow. And if you're thinking of hiking down and bringing the mules back, you'll have to figure on at least four days—if the weather warms up enough to melt this snow.'

'Lansford can't wait for the snow to melt,' Cordell said. 'He'd be in prison by then. And he doesn't need the mules. He's going to carry a quarter of a million dollars in bullion out on his back.'

'No,' Lansford said easily, 'not on my back. But I am going to carry it out. We have four sound horses. They can pack eight hundred pounds of gold among them.'

Maudie lifted the coffee pot lid and dropped coffee onto the boiling water. She said, 'Pack it where, Mont?'

She set the pot off the fire and added a little cold water to settle the grounds. Lansford said, 'If the only direction we can take horses is south, then we go south.'

Maudie gave him that wondering look again, but said nothing. Cordell watched her pour coffee into a cup and carry it to Lebow. Lansford and Blanton were watching her too and Cordell used this brief moment of not being guarded to test the ropes around his wrists. They were so tight that his flesh had swollen. He knew he had no chance to twist free.

He turned his attention to Maudie again. Lebow was watching her too, the gleam of life back in his eyes. But when she reached him, the gleam faded and he threw up his arms and legs in that same peculiar way that Cordell had found so remarkable.

The idea that had prowled the edge of

Cordell's mind before he fell asleep came close enough now for him to hold onto. The gold must be under the big rock! That would account for Lebow's insistence on sitting there, for his strange way of protecting the rock with his body whenever anyone approached him. He was like a mother bird trying to cover her precious eggs from the eyes of an intruder.

Cordell wondered why Lansford hadn't understood the meaning of Lebow's odd behavior. And he found the answer sourly amusing—the solution was too simple. Lansford had too complex a mind to see the simple truth. His own actions were so devious that he couldn't imagine anyone acting differently.

Lebow relaxed as Maudie waited patiently, holding the cup toward him. He leaned forward finally and took it from her. Lansford snapped his fingers as if he'd made a decision.

He said, 'All right, Sergeant, you told me before you knew how to make Lebow talk. Prove it now.'

Blanton grunted. 'It's about time you started using your head, Captain.' He strode to Lebow.

Lebow watched him for a moment without moving. Then he jerked his bound arms up. Hot coffee spilled onto his face and over his legs. He seemed not to notice. His face worked as Blanton came abreast of the rock.

'It's my gold!' Lebow shrieked.

91

'Where is it?' Blanton said with soft savagery. He reached for Lebow. 'You're going to tell me before I'm done with you. So make it easy on yourself and tell me now.'

'My gold!' Lebow cried. He threw the empty cup into Blanton's face.

Blanton swore. He wrapped both of his huge hands around Lebow's ankle and pulled. Lebow tumbled off the rock, kicking at Blanton with his free leg. Blanton elbowed the kick aside and grabbed Lebow by the front of his coat. He pulled until the rope running from Lebow's waist to the tree behind him was stretched taut.

Blanton held Lebow rigidly. 'You got two minutes to make up your mind,' he said in his deep, rumbling voice.

'Stop it!' Maudie cried. She looked beseechingly at Lansford. 'Mont, make him stop!'

Lansford looked at her and then at Lebow. 'I didn't go through hell for that gold just to let a fool balk me,' he said coldly.

Cordell saw the shock of full understanding reach Maudie. She lifted one hand slowly and pressed it against her lips. She stood that way, immobile, staring at Lansford. She dropped her hand suddenly and walked to the rear of the overhang, near where Cordell sat. She pressed her back against the rockwall, as if she needed its support.

She said stiffly, painfully, 'I'm sorry,

Lieutenant Cordell.'

Cordell said, 'Once Lansford realized he no longer needed the mules, he no longer needed to pretend to you either.'

'I know,' she whispered. 'I knew before—only I wouldn't admit it to myself.' She looked at him, her face without color, her eyes pleading for understanding.

Cordell looked beyond her, at the scene by the rock. 'It isn't important right now,' he said. His lips thinned out in anger as Blanton grasped Lebow's soft body and shook it roughly.

'Help me to my feet!' Cordell ordered Maudie in a soft voice.

She opened her mouth as if to ask a question. Then, without speaking, she bent and caught Cordell under the armpits. She pulled as he thrust with his legs. Slowly he came erect.

He twisted until he faced the rock. 'Give me an easy push.'

'You can't . . .'

'Push!' he repeated.

Maudie pushed. Cordell hopped at the same moment. His momentum carried him forward and he stayed erect as long as he kept hopping on his bound legs. He was almost to Lebow and Blanton when he felt his balance going. He had a glimpse of Lansford turning toward him. He gave a final lunge and threw himself sideways, into Lansford.

They went down together, Lansford cursing in shrill surprise. Cordell cried, 'Get a gun, Maudie!'

He heard her running toward them as he twisted, trying to pin Lansford down with his weight. Lansford worked an arm free and struck him cruelly on the side of the neck. Cordell rolled his head and butted downward, aiming for Lansford's face.

Heavy hands grabbed the back of his coat and lifted. He heard Blanton grunt and felt himself flung aside. He struck the hard ground and rolled. Maudie was still two strides from where the fight had taken place. She changed direction and went to her knees beside Cordell.

'I didn't think fast enough,' she said miserably. 'I . . .'

Cordell was looking at the sky over the treetops. He said, 'It doesn't make much difference. That's daylight coming out of the east. If I know Heddon, he'll be here as soon as there's light enough to see across the meadow.'

Blanton helped Lansford to his feet. He stepped back and looked toward the trees. 'He's right, Captain.'

Lansford brushed at his clothing. 'Every time Cordell mentions Heddon, you start to shake,' he said angrily. 'Now can you or can't you get Lebow to tell us where he put that gold of ours?'

'If Heddon's crew gets across the meadow and into these trees, all the gold in Arizona won't do us no good!' Blanton cried. He picked up a rifle and strode out of the camp.

Lansford watched him for a moment and then glanced at Maudie. 'Trying to help Cordell was a foolish thing to do,' he said.

She stared at him silently. Cordell glanced at both of them briefly before turning his attention back to the swiftly lightening sky.

Blanton burst into the clearing. 'They're coming, Captain. Five of 'em!' He ran to his pile of gear and rooted in it. He found a box of shells and jammed them into his pocket.

Lansford was staring now at Lebow.

'Captain, did you hear me?' Blanton shouted. 'Heddon is coming. He's part way across the meadow already! He'll be here in another ten or fifteen minutes!'

XI

Lansford took his eyes off Lebow. He sucked in a deep breath. 'All right,' he said calmly. 'Let's go shoot a few of your bogey men.'

He picked up a rifle and stopped. 'But first,' he ordered, 'get Cordell back where he was and tie his wrists behind him. I don't want to worry about attack from two directions.'

Blanton gave Lebow's ropes a quick examination and then moved to Cordell. Maudie stood up, facing Blanton defiantly. Cordell murmured, 'There's nothing you can do. Just keep out of their way.'

She held her position for a moment more and then walked to the overhang and remained still while Blanton half carried, half dragged Cordell back there and untied his wrists. Cordell made no effort to help or hinder Blanton. Lansford was being too watchful.

Blanton finished lashing Cordell's wrists behind his back and walked to the fire. He gathered up Cordell's rifle and handgun. 'I'll take these along just in case, Captain.'

'All right,' Lansford said. He was looking at Lebow again, his expression thoughtful.

Maudie whispered, 'Why didn't you fight when your hands were free?'

Cordell said, 'I'll have a better chance when

they're gone.' He spoke in a careful whisper. 'Look what Blanton lost out of his saddlebag when he was getting those shells.'

Maudie gave him a puzzled glance and then looked at the scatter of Blanton's gear. Cordell saw some of the tension run out of her and he knew she'd seen the same thing he'd noticed earlier—a large clasp knife lying half hidden beside Blanton's things.

'I'll bring you some coffee,' she said loudly.

Lansford gave her a sharp look. 'You won't have time. You're coming with us.'

'You better tie her up too, Captain,' Blanton objected. 'She's liable to backbite you right in the middle of the fight.'

'I'll risk that,' Lansford said quietly. He motioned at Maudie with his rifle. 'I'm going to try to bargain with Heddon. She might be of some use to us.'

Maudie stopped. Lansford twitched his rifle. 'Don't get the idea I won't use this on you,' he said coolly. 'Remember I came here to get a quarter of a million in gold. I don't intend to let anyone—not even you, my dear—stand in my way. Now move along!'

Maudie looked back at Cordell. He nodded his head gently. She turned away and walked rapidly into the trees. Lansford and Blanton followed.

Cordell sat quietly until the crackling of frozen brush died away. Then he toppled onto his side and rolled toward Blanton's gear at

97

the near side of the fire.

The ground was rough, with a slight upslope, and once Cordell thought he wasn't going to be able to force himself forward any farther. He lay belly down, rocking in an effort to build up momentum, and gaining nothing against the rise of the ground. Finally his toes and fingers found purchase and he went over onto his back. He kicked his legs up and forward, letting their weight pull him onto his belly again. After that, he was on level ground and he could roll again.

He reached Blanton's saddlebag and lay a moment resting. He could hear no sound from the direction of the meadow. But the light was spreading quickly over the sky, and he knew that once it reached the point where trees and rocks separated themselves into distinct shapes, Heddon and his crew would make their first rush.

Cordell rolled again, putting his back to the saddlebag. He groped until he found the heavy clasp knife.

Cordell grunted as the knife slipped away. He rocked back, scrabbling with his fingers. Then heard the first clear, sharp crack of a carbine. The air seemed to hang motionless, empty and still, so that even the cracklings from the fire faded away. Then two more carbine shots shattered the silence. The heavier roar of more powerful rifles rumbled off the surrounding cliffs in deep echocs. The shots rose to a crescendo and slacked off. Silence came down again.

Cordell worked carefully to get his thumbnail under the notch in the knife blade when his hands found it again.

He heard someone coming quickly through the trees and he tried to hide the knife in his fingers. Tension ran out of him as he saw Maudie. She stumbled a little as she came into the clearing. She was carrying Cordell's rifle, holding it across her breast with both hands.

She ran to him. 'Turn over,' she said. 'Hurry, please!'

Cordell rolled onto his belly and opened his hands so she could see the knife. He felt her take it from him. 'What happened?'

'Heddon's men can't ride very fast,' she said. 'The snow's too deep. But Mont didn't understand that. He started shooting before they were in good range. They shot back, but no one got hit.'

Cordell felt the ropes around his wrists give. He pulled his arms in front of him and flexed his fingers. 'Was Blanton right—there were five in Heddon's party?'

Maudie nodded. She sawed at his ankle ropes.

'How did you get away?' Cordell asked.

'When Heddon started shooting, Mont turned his back on me. Blanton had to set your rifle down and he was too busy sighting his own to bother with me. So I picked up your gun and ran.'

More shots came, slow and evenly spaced. There was no answering fire. Cordell listened intently and then got to his feet. He stamped around, driving the needles from his cramped legs.

'You were just lucky,' Cordell said. 'Don't be so foolhardy again.'

Maudie said nothing but looked pointedly at Lebow. Cordell understood her meaning. 'Leave him for now. I don't want him hurt any more than you do. But he isn't predictable. He's safer where he is than anywhere else around here.'

He nodded at the knife she held in her hand. 'Keep that with you. And take some food and a horse if you can. You know this country. Maybe you can figure a way out and get home.'

Cordell left her staring around the camp as if trying to decide what to take with her. He hurried through the forest, carrying his carbine. Shots came only occasionally now but there were enough to give him Lansford and Blanton's position. He angled to their left and stopped at the edge of the meadow. He estimated that he was a good thirty feet east of them.

The sky was very light now and Cordell could see the meadow clearly. He located Pike Heddon at once. He was leading a broken line of riders zig-zag through the heavy snow in

100

such a fashion that none of them made a solid target.

At the same time, Cordell knew, before long the distance between Heddon and the forest would be too close for any maneuver to keep him from being an easy mark for a bullet. Cordell frowned and shook his head. Pike Heddon was noted for his strategy, his Indianlike generalship; yet he was riding boldly in the open as casually as if Lansford and Blanton weren't sniping at him, as if there was nothing ahead of him but the timber.

Cordell sensed a trick, but as hard as he stared, he could see nothing to indicate one. He settled down to wait for Heddon to get into better range.

Heddon came on. Cordell lifted his gun and took careful aim. This was no time for the niceties of the law. Heddon would kill him as quickly as he'd kill Lansford and Blanton. But when he fired, he aimed at Heddon's shoulder. It wasn't in him to shoot to kill, unless he was fired on first himself.

Lansford and Blanton shot at that moment too. Snow spurted between the advancing horses as their riders swung them in that zigzag pattern. Heddon stopped and raised his gun. His men copied him. They fired almost in unison. The bullets went high, ticking through the trees.

Heddon lowered his rifle and raised a hand. He swung his horse around and retreated, working back through the snow he and his crew had broken with their advance.

Cordell stepped into the open to get a better shot at Heddon. Movement caught his side vision. He pivoted to his left in time to see dim shadows flowing across the face of the rock wall that hemmed the meadow in the northeast.

Men on foot creeping to the far edge of the forest! Cordell understood Heddon's strategy, knew why he'd had four of his men with him in the open. The riders had been decoys to draw the attention of such lookouts as the camp might have posted. While the riders feigned an attack, the others would filter into the trees. Then they could either take the camp by surprise or keep its defenders busy while the five on horseback rode in unhindered.

Cordell lifted his rifle and fired at the shadowy movement. Then he shouted, 'Lansford! Blanton! To the north-east!' He fired again.

He heard Blanton's bull-like roar of surprise. He glanced west to see both men standing in the open, raking the shadows with their guns. A dark form hurtled into the meadow, a man running in a crazy, pain-filled pattern. He fell suddenly, only to rise again and stagger in the direction of the cut.

Blanton sent a bullet kicking snow near the running man's feet. 'Save your lead!' Cordell shouted. 'They're going now.'

Blanton disappeared into the forest.

The other figures had stumbled out of the shadows and were struggling through the snow after the wounded man. The riders picked up their pace as well, moving eastward. Cordell looked away from them and probed the rock shadows with his eyes, seeking further movement there.

Maudie's voice cried, 'Watch out behind you!'

Cordell twisted around. He saw Blanton lining his rifle on him not twenty feet away. He threw himself toward the trees, just as Blanton fired. The bullet jarred his leg as it whipped a corner from his boot heel. Blanton fired again, but Cordell was rolling, and the bullet thunked harmlessly into the snow.

Blanton turned and sifted into the shadows, out of sight.

Cordell crawled behind a tree and got to his feet. Maudie stood in the open a few feet away.

'Thanks. But I told you not to be foolhardy again. Now get out of here before one of them finds you and shoots you.'

Maudie stood where she was, looking at him. A frozen twig snapped loudly on the cold air; the sound came from the direction of the camp.

'Hurry up!' Cordell commanded.

Maudie remained where she was, peering into the shadows. 'I won't leave alone,' she said flatly. 'I'll meet you on the rocks above the overhang.'

Cordell's rising anger was checked by a brief glimpse of Lansford moving quickly toward them, hiding himself behind first one tree and then another. Maudie gasped as she saw him too.

'Well, it's too late now,' Cordell said bitterly. 'Lansford is between us and the camp.'

'I can lose him,' Maudie said and ran into the trees before Cordell could protest.

Cordell saw Lansford's head come up at the sound of her running. The dark, quick man loped after her.

Cordell swore as he realized Maudie was trying to protect him by leading Lansford away. Angrily, he stepped into the open and snapped a shot at Lansford. Bark flew and then Lansford was out of sight. Cordell moved after him, fighting deep snow until he came to a small cleared spot.

A crackling of brush turned him to the left as he reached firmer footing. He tried to bring his gun around with him but a tree branch caught him, jerking the gun out of his hand.

Cordell stared at Blanton who was just six feet away. Blanton brought his rifle up slowly, lining it on the broad expanse of Cordell's chest.

'I've been waiting quite a while for this,' Blanton said.

XII

Blanton levered a shell into his rifle. Cordell left his feet in a twisting dive as Blanton's gun made a hard, cracking sound. Frozen forest duff spattered stingingly into Cordell's face.

Cordell hit the snow at Blanton's feet and rolled as Blanton jumped back and drove the rifle butt savagely toward his head. Cordell hooked out an arm, catching Blanton's ankle.

Blanton came down on top of him, swearing and reaching for his hand gun. Cordell got both hands on Blanton's wrist. They rolled through the thin snow, brittle bushes crackling sharply under their weight. Blanton's fingers were inches from his gun butt, held away by the force of Cordell's grip.

'Don't be a fool,' Cordell grunted. 'We have Heddon to fight.'

'I don't aim to watch out for Heddon and you at the same time,' Blanton panted. He twisted his arm, jerking it free of Cordell's fingers and bringing his gun out of its holster.

Cordell lashed out with a foot as Blanton moved away. Cordell's boot-heel struck Blanton's wrist, sending the gun skittering through the snow. Both men reached their feet at the same time. Cordell was closer to the gun and he kicked at it, driving it out of sight into a patch of brush.

He straightened up as Blanton came at him in a savage rush.

Blanton was a powerful man and he brought his weight as well as the force of his rush into a tremendous swing of his fist. Cordell was off balance and even the glancing jolt of Blanton's fist against his cheek sent him spinning backward. His back came up sharply against the bole of a tree, driving the wind from his lungs. He hung there, almost falling to the ground, helpless as Blanton came at him again.

Blanton slowed his rush and moved in warily, his eyes on Cordell's face. Cordell found his breath and felt strength flow back into his muscles. He let himself sag, hoping to take advantage of Blanton's cautious approach. He had no chance at all if Blanton hit him again. The man might be hungry and cold and tired, but he moved with an easy quickness, swinging his powerful shoulders, shifting his feet like a man trained in fighting.

Cordell put both hands behind him, bracing them against the rough tree trunk. Blanton made a sudden charge, ducking and weaving as he came. Cordell lifted his leg and thrust backward with his hands. His booted foot drove forward like a battering ram. Blanton tried to turn away from the blow, but it caught him on the hipbone and spun him off balance.

Cordell pushed himself forward. He hit Blanton in the mouth, knocking him off his feet. Blanton rolled and tried to get up.

Cordell lifted a knee into his face, smashing his nose. Blanton went backward, rolled over, and lay with his face in the scuffed snow.

Cordell wiped blood off his cheek where Blanton's knuckles had broken the skin. He stood panting, his eyes searching for Blanton's handgun. He saw it a few feet away and he stepped toward it.

Lansford's voice came softly: 'Stay where you are, Cordell.'

He stood close to where Cordell had dropped his rifle. He held his own gun at hip height. Cordell judged his chance of reaching Lansford across fifteen feet of space and dismissed it.

'Help Blanton up and back to camp,' Lansford said. His voice was almost amiable. 'It looks like we start all over again, doesn't it?'

Cordell said, 'I didn't know you were so shortsighted, Lansford. There'll be another attack and you'll need all the guns you can get.'

'I'll be gone before the fools make up their minds what to do next,' Lansford said softly. 'Lebow is through being stubborn.'

Cordell felt a chill at the undertone in Lansford's voice. He looked across the space between them. The first sunlight slanted into the trees, touching Lansford's features, showing the cold light in his eyes. Cordell turned away and walked back to Blanton.

He bent down and slid his hands under

107

Blanton's armpits. He grunted as he straightened, lifting the heavier man with him. Blanton was unconscious, a soggy weight that strained the muscles in Cordell's arms.

Cordell shifted his grip, sliding his hands forward and gripping his fingers into Blanton's bulky coatfront. He pivoted slowly, awkwardly as if he was having trouble holding Blanton upright.

'Rub snow in his face. That'll bring him around,' Lansford said lightly.

Cordell took a deep breath and jerked so that Blanton's body came up to its full height. He braced his boot heels and heaved forward, throwing Blanton at Lansford. The same instant, he turned and ran, plunging through waist high brush and on toward the thicker part of the forest.

He glanced back to see Lansford lift his rifle and fire. The shot went wide, ticking a branch well to Cordell's right. Lansford ran at Blanton and drove a boot into his side.

'Get up, you fool!' he screamed. 'Get up and find Cordell! Find him and kill him!'

So Lansford's control had finally broken, Cordell realized wonderingly. Lansford's only thought right now must be that he had both Heddon and Cordell to worry about while he tried to force Lebow into giving him the gold. Lansford seemed to have forgotten that he and Blanton had all the guns. That Cordell could be hunted at their leisure.

But he would remember it soon enough, Cordell thought as he ran on through the cold, silent forest.

He worked his way slowly through the trees, seeking some sign of Maudie. He finally realized he'd circled near the camp when he stumbled into a clearing holding the horses—his buckskin and the four Lansford had brought.

The buckskin whinnied, pulling at its stake in an effort to get to Cordell. He heard a deep-voiced cry, 'Come on, Captain, that'll be Cordell with the horses now!'

A heavy body crashed through the brush toward the clearing. Cordell limped swiftly in the opposite direction, staying on wind cleared ground to keep his prints from showing.

After a time he rested. The sounds of two men moving through the brush came faintly from behind and to his right. He went on again. Suddenly he found himself at the far end of a long tongue of timber. It stretched out from the main body of the forest to within fifty yards of the west cut Blanton had talked about.

Cordell thought that with luck he could work his way across the thin snow and buck through the cut to safety. He looked at it for a long while; then he turned back to search for Maudie again.

He made a wide swing to the north and east, stopping when the sheer rock wall blocked him. The crackling of frozen brush gave warning that Blanton and Lansford were closing in on him. He grimaced. He had no choice but to work back toward the camp. If he left the trees for the open meadow, Heddon's men would spot him. If he waited where he was or tried to go back the way he'd just come, he would run into Lansford or Blanton.

He moved slowly south and west. He stopped now and then to examine the sheer cliff face, hoping to find some hiding place in that implacable wall of stone. The crackling of brush was closer now, directly to his left, and he quickened his pace.

He smelled smoke from the campfire at the same time he saw a great jumble of boulders directly ahead. He hurried forward, eager to know if the boulders would give him some refuge from the relentless pursuit coming closer.

His nerves jumped as he saw a dirty pad of snow by a narrow passage between two rocks on his right. He leaned forward, squeezing himself into the passage. Beyond it, a narrow ledge slanted upward along the cliff face, and here he could see sign left by Maudie. The ledge went westerly, toward the camp.

This was what she'd meant about meeting him above the overhang, he realized. Quickly, he wormed his heavy shoulders through the narrow passage and pulled himself to the ledge. He turned around and leaned down until he had smoothed away any sign he and Maudie might have left.

He crawled up a narrow crevasse, the ledge making a path a dozen feet above the pinched bottom of the crevasse. The ledge widened abruptly and Cordell came out into the bright glare of sunshine. He looked in surprise at the westerly slant of the sun. He'd spent a good part of the day looking for Maudie and evading Lansford and Blanton!

Cordell followed the ledge around a wide upthrust of rock. The upthrust broke away suddenly and he found himself looking across the overhang and down into the camp. It was empty.

He lifted his head and saw Maudie sitting in a small space she'd brushed clear of snow. She beckoned to him, a finger to her lips. Cordell crawled to a position beside her, and from this angle he could see Lansford and Blanton coming slowly through the trees and into the camp.

He relaxed. He wasn't concerned with being seen from below. As long as the sun stayed above the rimrock, it shone down on the snow cover here with such brilliance that anyone looking upward would be blinded by the glare.

Blanton went directly to the fire and stood warming himself. His face was puffed and his nose swollen from his fight with Cordell. Fresh blood ran from a cut in his lower lip and he daubed at it with a soiled bandana. Lansford came up and put water on to heat. Blanton turned his head slowly.

'Don't you ever lay a hand on me again, Captain,' he said in a quiet voice. 'I'm staying with you because there's no place else to go.' He jerked his head toward the rock where Lebow sat buried in his strange apathy. Dried blood streaked his face, showing Cordell that Blanton had been trying to force him to talk again.

'You want to take your mad at Cordell out on somebody, Captain, use Lebow. Maybe you can get him to talk.'

'Not by beating, I won't,' Lansford said. 'And neither will you.' There was no apology to Blanton in his curt voice.

He turned and looked at Lebow. 'But I know how to handle him now,' he said. 'Tend to the coffee.'

He walked to the rock. Lebow shrank back but made no other move. Lansford spoke to him in a voice too low for Cordell to hear. He returned to the campfire and nodded at Blanton.

'I told him what to expect,' Lansford said. 'He has an hour to think it over.'

'Have we got an hour to spare, Captain?' Blanton demanded.

Lansford said thoughtfully, 'I don't think Heddon will attack until dusk. His strategy went wrong. He'll wait for another chance to catch us off guard.'

112

He smiled almost amiably, walked to Blanton's pile of gear and picked up a short folding shovel. He laid it carefully on rocks near the fire so that just the metal blade was close to the coals.

Maudie stifled a gasp. She whispered to Cordell, 'Oh, no! He can't want anything badly enough to—to torture for it.'

'Lansford's desperate,' Cordell replied in a low voice. 'He's lost control of himself. Heddon is pressing him and he isn't sure where I am. And he knows he went too far with Blanton.'

Maudie whispered desperately, 'Can't Mont see where the gold is?'

'You know then?' Cordell murmured.

'I've known since the first time I saw the way that poor man clung to his rock,' she answered.

Cordell glanced at Lebow. He was paying no attention to anything around him.

'Maybe he'll tell before Mont hurts him badly,' Maudie said hopefully.

Cordell shook his head. 'He might have once, but not any longer. Even when he was rational, he risked angering Lansford to keep the gold himself. And now he isn't rational. He'll probably let himself be killed before he tells.'

'He's—insane?'

'Not all the time,' Cordell said. 'He has moments when he's aware of the world around him. But I think the shock of what's happened to him has been too great. It's as if he's crawled into a strange dark cave. Some other shock may bring him out of it, but not soon enough to keep Lansford from torturing him.'

He looked from Lebow to the fire. Blanton was gulping down a cup of coffee. He finished, picked up his carbine, and started for the trees. 'Heddon may wait for dusk,' he said, 'But I'm taking a look to make sure.'

He walked out of sight. Lansford shrugged and studied the slowly reddening tip of the shovel he'd placed in the fire.

Cordell turned his attention to the sky. The sun was starting its last swift slide toward the rimrock and darkness. Soon there would be no glare on the snow here to protect him and Maudie. And soon too, he thought, Pike Heddon would have another plan ready to put into action.

The entire meadow was visible from the ledge and Cordell looked toward the east cut to see if there was any activity there. While he watched, two riders appeared. They spent a moment in huddled consultation and then started their horses westward. Four other men appeared, watched the riders a moment, and then disappeared back into the cut.

In the camp, Lansford poured himself coffee and sipped it, his eyes fixed on the tip of the shovel. It was turning an ugly, angry red.

Maudie whispered, 'Isn't there something

we can do?'

Cordell didn't answer at once. His mind was busy visualizing Heddon's strategy. When he spoke, his voice was sour, 'It's too late to make much difference. You saw those two horsemen. Heddon must have sent them to seal off the west cut. They'll reach it in an hour. Then, even if Lansford gets the gold, he won't have any place to take it.'

He glanced at the dimming sunlight. 'And he won't have any place to go to get away from Heddon. None of us will.'

XIII

Futile anger filled Cordell. Without a gun, he was helpless to even try to stop Heddon's men from sealing off the west cut. Once that happened, Heddon wouldn't have to risk an attack. All he had to do was wait for them to starve.

Cordell's thoughts were bleak. This meant his mission would fail. But that didn't bother him as much as he expected. Because Heddon's new move meant death for all of them—even Maudie. Pike Heddon couldn't risk letting one of them get away to tell what had happened.

A thin scream rose from the camp, jerking Cordell's attention back to the scene below him. Lansford was standing at the base of the rock, holding the glowing shovel tip up for Lebow to see. Lebow stared at Lansford with no realization on his face.

Lansford's voice was clear, 'Are you ready to tell me where the gold is?'

Lebow repeated in a thick voice, 'Gold?' His body jerked out into that strange protective posture. 'It's my gold!' he cried.

Lansford thrust the shovel closer, stopping it inches from Lebow's face. Lebow screamed again and tried to pull away, but the rope running from his waist to the tree held him.

116

Cordell surged to his feet. Maudie caught his arm in an effort to pull him down. 'You'll only be shot!' she whispered frantically. 'Let me try to stop Mont.'

She jerked with surprising strength, putting him off balance. Before he'd recovered, she was past him and running along the ledge. He started after her. Caution caught him and he stopped abruptly. Maudie was right. If he went down there he was asking for recapture and death.

He turned his eyes back to Lansford. He was holding the shovel about a foot from Lebow's leg now, the red tip steady. Then the shovel edged forward.

'Talk! Do you hear me? Talk!'

Lebow stared at him blankly.

Maudie burst from the trees and ran into the camp. 'Stop it!' she pleaded. 'What kind of an animal are you? Can't you see Lebow is mad?'

Lansford pulled the shovel back and faced Maudie.

'If you don't like what I'm doing, go ask Cordell for help.' He laughed at her. 'Find out how much use he is without a gun!'

He turned away to lift the shovel again. Maudie said, 'You're wasting time, Mont. Two of Heddon's men are crossing the meadow to seal off the west cut. I saw them. It won't be long before you won't have anywhere to go with your gold.'

'Don't be childish,' he said in his arrogant voice. 'I'm not Blanton. I don't frighten easily.' He extended the shovel tip again. A heavy crashing to his right made him pause and look at the trees. Blanton lumbered into camp, leading the horses.

'Captain,' he panted, 'two of Heddon's men are riding west. They mean to trap us in here. But we can beat them if we ride out now.'

Lansford didn't move for a long minute. Then he pushed the shovel closer to Lebow. 'If that's the case,' he said in a rigidly calm voice, 'I've no more time to waste.'

His voice turned sharp. 'Sergeant, tie Maudie up. I don't want to be interfered with. And then start packing. We're over halfway to the west cut here. If we hurry, we might be able to get through before we're cut off.'

He thrust the shovel directly at Lebow's face. 'Now talk!' he shouted.

Lebow shrank sideways wildly and lost his balance. His hands flailed in the air. He slid, screamed as the rope about his waist jerked him, cascading him up and out. He hit the ground with a soggy thump and lay still.

Maudie ran to him with a soft cry. She pulled the clasp knife from her pocket and slashed at the ropes around his wrists. Blanton swore and ran to her. She whirled and slashed the knife at him. He ducked the glittering blade and struck her with the flat of his hand, knocking her backward. The knife flew from

118

her fingers.

Cordell's anger shattered in a great blinding burst. He picked up a fist-sized rock and stepped to the lip of the overhang, and threw it. Even though he recognized the futility of his action, there was some satisfaction in it for its own sake.

The rock struck Blanton's leg. He swung around, his gun lifting. Maudie shouted, 'No! Get back! Get back!' and staggered into Blanton, sending him to his knees.

Lansford drew his hand gun and fired wildly at the snow above the overhang. Both shots spattered snow a few feet from Cordell. He ducked back, flattening himself on the ledge, swearing at his own helplessness.

Blanton surged up, his fingers twisted in the collar of Maudie's jacket. 'Help me tie this wildcat, Captain, and then I'll go after Cordell.'

Lansford found a piece of rope and whipped it around Maudie's wrists. He ran a loop to her ankles and drew it tight. She fell to the ground on her side.

'Let her lie there,' Lansford said coldly. 'And forget about Cordell. He isn't armed. He can't do anything to us, and we have no time to waste on him.'

He picked up the knife Maudie had dropped and walked to where Lebow lay. He scooped a handful of snow and rubbed it viciously into Lebow's face. As Lebow's eyes

119

opened, Lansford pressed the point of the knife to his throat. Lebow seemed unaware of Lansford. His gaze was off in space, his lips were slack.

'Leave him alone,' Maudie cried. 'I'll tell you where the gold is if you'll leave him alone.'

Lansford lifted the knife point slightly. 'What kind of a trick is this?'

'It's no trick,' she said. 'The gold is under the big rock Lebow was sitting on.'

Blanton swore in surprise. He strode to the rock and drove the butt of his rifle into the dirt at the base. The rifle butt broke through the thin frozen crust and into softer dirt beneath.

'By God, Captain, I think she's right! We figured Lebow's climbing up there was his crazy way of trying to keep out of our reach. But that wasn't it at all.'

A flush touched Lansford's cheeks. He said, 'We'll see. The shovel's cooled off, Sergeant. Take it and start digging.'

Cordell watched Blanton probe the ground with the shovel, seeking the best place to dig. He looked up occasionally to check the progress of Heddon's men across the meadow. They moved slowly, fighting drifts chest high to their horses, making a wide southerly swing to keep out of range of any sniper who might be stationed in the trees.

They were still a good distance from the west cut, and Cordell judged that they still had close to an hour of hard riding before they'd get there.

He heard Blanton's triumphant cry and looked down to see dirt flying from the shovel. Blanton stopped digging and went to his knees. He reached into the hole he'd scooped under the rook and brought out a grimy double-sewn canvas sack.

'Here it is, Captain!' He threw the sack aside and brought out another. Lansford knelt beside him and helped.

When the last sack lay above the ground, Blanton shouted, 'Look at that, Captain! A quarter of a million dollars.'

Lansford got to his feet. Lebow was staring at the pile of sacks. His face worked and he cried like a child.

Lansford said, 'Let's load the horses, Sergeant. We'll take Maudie with us.' He jerked his head at Lebow. 'Heddon can have him—for what he's worth.'

Cordell heard the triumph in Lansford's voice, noted the arrogant confidence coming back into him. He wondered if Lansford really believed he could still escape.

Cordell shouted down, 'Heddon's men are closer to the cut, Lansford. You haven't got a chance of getting there first. If you want to risk your own neck, go ahead, but don't force Maudie to go with you.'

Lansford squinted upward into the still lingering glare of the sun. 'It happens that I have a use for the lady,' his voice mocked

Cordell. 'If you're so concerned, join us. Maybe you can protect her by throwing snowballs at Heddon's men.'

Blanton grabbed up his rifle and tried to find Cordell. He lifted the gun and sent a quick spray of shots upward. Cordell flattened himself on the snow as the bullets ranged close above him.

Lansford said sharply, 'Save your ammunition, Sergeant. Cordell is all noise and no weapon. Let's get these horses loaded.'

Cordell looked around himself. There wasn't even another loose rock close by him. Once he started down the ledge, then stopped. As long as he was free and alive, he had some hope. Letting himself be recaptured now would be the same as signing his own death warrant—and Maudie's.

He forced himself to stillness, watching as Blanton worked skillfully, tying two gold sacks onto a piece of rope just long enough to go over a horse's back and rest the sacks on the saddle skirts. The last horse, Cordell's buckskin, had only half a load and so Blanton used him to pack the necessary camp gear.

When the horses were ready, Lansford cut Maudie's ankles loose and ran a long rope from her waist to the buckskin's saddle.

She watched him with no sign of fear. Lansford finished checking the knot around her waist, stepped back and bowed mockingly.

'What do you want with me?' she

122

demanded. 'You've got your gold.'

'Once you show us the trail to Mexico, you're free to go, my dear.'

Maudie looked around slowly, her eyes stopping at Lebow. 'And you're really leaving him to that man Heddon—to be slaughtered?'

Lansford laughed. 'Maybe Cordell will rescue him.'

He turned to Blanton. 'All right, Sergeant, let's get moving!'

XIV

A spire of rock marked the end of the ledge. Cordell hurried there as soon as the pack-train disappeared into the trees. He climbed to a point where he could follow the progress of the line of horses toward the lower end of the meadow.

Blanton and his horse were leading the string. He chose his route carefully, keeping out of sight of anyone in the meadow and at the same time staying out of deep brush and areas of deep snow. Cordell saw that he was making as direct a line as possible toward the tongue of timber that reached to within fifty yards of the west cut.

Lansford walked along beside the third horse in the string. Now and then he glanced back at Maudie who trailed the buckskin at the end of a fairly long rope. Cordell felt a surge of pleasure in the way she walked, head up and shoulders straight, the dignity of her bearing taking the sting from Lansford's contemptuous cruelty.

Cordell turned his attention to the meadow. The two riders working their way toward the west cut had run into drifts so deep they were forced to buck ahead, fall back, and buck ahead again to make any progress. Watching them, Cordell judged that now the pack-train had a fair chance of reaching the cut first.

The sun slid behind the west rimrock, deepening and spreading the shadows over the face of the meadow. Cordell glanced eastward, anxious to see if he could tell what Pike Heddon's next move would be.

He saw one man on foot at the mouth of the east cut. The other five formed a huddled group on horseback nearby. While Cordell watched, the unmistakable figure of Heddon broke from the group and started along the northeast edge of the meadow toward the trees. The other riders fell in line behind him, leaving the man on foot to guard the cut.

Cordell grunted as he realized the meaning of this latest move. Heddon would be hoping that any lookout Lansford might have posted would be distracted by the two men riding westward, and that he and his remaining crew could slip through the shadows to the timber.

Cordell looked again at the slowly moving pack-train. Once Heddon found the empty camp, he would need little time to find out what had happened. He'd go after Lansford, and he'd have no trouble catching up with the pack-train. Then he could attack from the rear while the other two riders pinned it down in front.

And Maudie would be helpless.

Cordell saw that his only hope of saving Maudie lay in delaying Heddon. If he could do that for even a quarter of an hour, the pack-train might get close enough to the cut for Lansford and Blanton to fight their way through to the safety of the other side. If he could get Heddon and his crew into the abandoned campsite and hold them there somehow for those precious minutes, Maudie might reach safety.

He gave little thought now to Lansford's capture, and less to the gold. His immediate concern was for Maudie Ellison.

*   *   *

Cordell climbed hurriedly higher on the spire of rock. He worked his way along a narrow lip of rock until he was directly in line with Heddon and his riders to the northeast. The air grew cold as the shadows lengthened. Cordell clung to his perch and cursed Heddon for not looking in his direction.

He moved slowly along the lip of rock, deliberately outlining himself against the snow at different angles. Heddon was almost to the far edge of the timber when Cordell saw him stop, lift an arm, and point. Cordell held motionless until there was no doubt Heddon had located him.

Quickly now, Cordell dropped to the ledge. He ran along it to the overhang, slid down its slope, and jumped the dozen feet to the ground. He went to his knees, gasping as the jolt ran up into his wounded thigh. When he

126

was able to stand again, he turned his attention to Lebow.

While Cordell was on the spire of rock, Lebow had been out of sight. Cordell saw now that he had moved only enough to get to his knees. He was squeezing his bound hands between his legs, shivering in the cooling air. The fire was down to a few coals and threw no warmth to Lebow.

If Lebow felt the cold, Cordell thought hopefully, he might be ready to crawl from his dark cave back to understanding. Hurrying to him and untying the rope around his waist, Cordell led him to the fire. Cordell worked quickly, throwing all the wood he could find close by on the coals.

Flames leaped up as the fire sprang onto the new wood. Lebow raised his hands to shield his eyes and moved back. Cordell helped him to a spot under the overhang where he could absorb the heat reflected from the rock behind him.

Lebow sat with his head down, his body shivering until it drew enough of the fire's warmth into itself. Then he lifted his head and his eyes gleamed with flickering signs that he was trying to crawl back to life.

He said suddenly in an almost normal voice, 'There was a girl here? She gave me coffee, didn't she?'

'Yes.'

'Where is she?' Lebow demanded.

'Lansford took her,' Cordell said. He told Lebow briefly what had happened; what Lebow remembered had no more form than a dream. While he talked, he freed Lebow's wrists.

Lebow beat his hands against his legs. 'Why didn't you do something for her?' he demanded. 'Why did you let Lansford take her away—and the gold too?'

'He and Blanton have my guns,' Cordell replied.

Lebow stared at the fire. 'Did you say that Pike Heddon was coming here?'

'That's right,' Cordell said. 'He'll see this big fire and be on us before long. So it's time we got moving.' He took the rope that had been around Lebow's waist and looped it over his own shoulder.

Lebow started to get up and then sank back. 'What difference does it make?' he said. 'I'm nothing without the gold. It doesn't matter if Heddon finds me here or if I go back to the nothing I had before.'

Cordell chose his words carefully. 'It makes this much difference. I want to try to keep Heddon here until the pack-train has a chance to get out of the meadow.' He went to the big rock and pushed the dirt back in the hole, hiding as best he could the signs of the gold having been dug up.

'Let Heddon have the pack-train!' Lebow cried. 'Let him kill Lansford!'

'If he kills Lansford, he'll kill the girl, too,' Cordell said.

Lebow's eyes glinted suddenly. 'The girl,' he repeated. 'She was good to me, wasn't she?' He clenched his thick fingers. 'I want to help her for that. And I want to hurt Lansford and Blanton—the way they hurt me.'

He looked squarely at Cordell. 'But what can we do against Heddon? We have no guns and no horses.'

'I let Heddon see me,' Cordell said. 'If he thinks we're all still in camp, he'll come here. If we can keep him thinking that for fifteen minutes, the pack-train will have its chance.'

He started for the trees. 'Come on,' he commanded. 'Heddon will be here any minute.'

Lebow hesitated. Then he rose and followed Cordell. As they reached the trees, the crackle of the fire faded enough for Cordell to hear another sound—the sharp noise of riders pushing their way through frozen brush.

Cordell motioned for Lebow to hurry. Lebow moved awkwardly, still stiff from having been tied so long. Watching him move cautiously forward, Cordell wondered how long it would be until something happened to send Lebow back into his dark empty hole. They reached shelter behind the spire of rock and Cordell ordered Lebow to stop. Lebow sat down, breathing gustily through his open mouth.

A sudden burst of noise came from below telling Cordell that Heddon and his men were close to the camp. He looked anxiously at Lebow to see how this threat affected him.

Lebow showed no change and Cordell said quickly, 'Stay where you are. I'm going to find someplace where I can watch the camp and the meadow without exposing myself.'

He worked his way past the base of the spire. Some distance beyond he found a rounded rock that sloped sharply down to the forest thirty feet below. From its top he could see into the meadow and the farther part of the campsite. He climbed up, balancing himself precariously on the slippery, rounded surface.

The last of the evening light gave him a faint glimpse of the pack-train. It was nearly to the end of the tongue of timber now. Soon it would be in the open, away from the protective screen of trees, and in full view of Heddon's two riders.

Cordell watched them now as they bucked their horses through the deep drifts. The pack-train moved slowly, but had the advantage of going through thinner snow. It might reach the cut first.

If, Cordell thought, Lansford and Blanton could outshoot the riders and if he could hold Heddon back those final precious minutes, Maudie would be safe.

The sounds of Heddon's approach faded, then stopped altogether. Cordell felt his excitement rise. Heddon was apparently thinking in terms of an ambush and being very cautious.

An idea struck Cordell. 'It might work!' he whispered to himself. 'It might just work.'

Hurriedly he took the loop of rope from his shoulder and let one end drop down the side of the rock to the dark forest below. He reached up and tied the other end of the rope to a projection of stone above and to his left. A quick tug told him that the rope would hold a man's weight for a short time at least.

He slipped off the rock and worked his way back to Lebow. He said quickly, 'Heddon will be in camp soon. I want you to step out on the ledge where he can see you.'

Lebow stared at him. 'Why should I help you?' he demanded. 'If we get away from here, you'll only take the gold and put me in jail.'

'That's right,' Cordell agreed. 'But I'll put Blanton and Lansford in jail too.'

Lebow said almost slyly, 'I might kill them. I might take the gold away from you.'

'You might,' Cordell said. 'But I'll worry about that after Maudie Ellison is safe.'

Mention of Maudie seemed to stir something deep inside Lebow. He said, 'The girl.' His heavy lips twitched in an oddly shy smile. 'I'd like to take her away from Lansford,' he added.

'Then help me,' Cordell said bluntly. He waited for Lebow's assent and when it came, he spoke quickly, outlining his plan. Lebow stood up and looked toward that part of the ledge above the overhang.

He said, 'I'll try.'

Cordell left him, backtracking to the rounded rock. He crouched down in deep shadow, positioning himself so he could still see part of the camp.

The darkness in the timber thickened and Cordell looked hopefully for some sign of the rising moon. But the black sky held only the icy pinpricks of the stars. Cordell shivered as the cold mountain night clamped down, working its way through his clothing, stiffening his muscles.

Pike Heddon burst into view in the camp. He was on foot, his gun in his hand. He stared around the empty clearing, at the leaping flames of the fire.

'They tricked us!' he shouted. 'They've gone!'

Cordell whispered into the air, 'Now, Lebow! Now, before he's sure he's right and rides after Lansford!'

Cordell could see none of the ledge and less than half of the campsite, but he didn't need to see. Heddon's reaction told him what was happening.

Heddon lifted his arm, pointing in the direction of the ledge. 'There's Lebow—

up there!'

He leaped back into the trees. His voice boomed out excitedly as he issued orders, sending two men east to hunt for a way onto the ledge, sending two others west for the same purpose. He detailed himself to stay close to the camp, to watch the horses and to guard the area above the overhang.

As his men dispersed, he shouted, 'Watch for a trick. That government man, Cordell, is around somewhere.'

Cordell waited tensely, listening to the movements of Heddon's men through the forest and searching the darkness for some sign of the pack-train.

He saw it as it emerged from the blackness of the trees into the openness of the meadow. Starlight glinted on metal as Heddon's riders stopped their horses and lifted their guns. The sharp, flat crack of two rifles carried loudly on the cold, thin air.

Cordell saw Blanton drop to the snow. He bounded up and wrapped the reins of the lead horse around his waist. He plunged boldly toward the cut, forcing the horses to follow. Each few steps he paused just long enough to lift his carbine and snap a shot at the riders.

Lansford left his position and dropped quickly to the rear of the pack-train. Cordell swore as he saw Lansford screen himself behind Maudie and start firing. She darted forward suddenly, stopping when she was almost to the buckskin. She dropped flat until the horses moved enough to take up the slack in her rope. Then she climbed to her feet again, repeated her run, and dropped once more into the slender protection of the churned snow. Lansford moved up behind her, ignoring her maneuver as he kept up a steady firing.

A shout from the direction of the ledge sent Cordell hurrying back to the spire of rock. Lebow was crouched in shadow at its base. A lanky man stood on the ledge directly above the overhang. He was pointing toward the meadow.

'It's them, Pike!' he called over the crackle of rifle fire. 'It's Lansford and Blanton with a pack-train.' His voice shrilled up in a curse. 'They got Bert! They've drove Pete back out of range, away from the cut. They're going to get away sure!'

Heddon's voice roared up angrily. 'That means they've got the gold. That's why Lebow and Cordell are still here. Lansford found a way to leave them behind—for us. And they ain't got guns or Cordell wouldn't be around here. He'd be after Lansford.'

He nearly choked on his own fury. 'Cordell tricked us into coming here so Lansford'd have a better chance of getting away. I don't know why, but that's what he did, by God. Tom, you and Art come with me. We'll get Lansford yet. Slim, you and Runt keep looking for Lebow

134

and Cordell. And when you find 'em, shoot! We don't need Lebow no more to tell us where the gold is.'

The man on the ledge turned and moved swiftly in the direction of the spire of rock. Firelight leaped up, glinting off the gun in his hands. Cordell touched Lebow's shoulder.

'Come on,' he whispered. 'We haven't got a chance up here.'

Lebow got up and followed Cordell clumsily back to the rounded rock. Cordell showed him the rope. 'You'll have about a ten foot drop at the end. Make it as quiet as you can.'

He looked back at the camp. Two men were running in. They reached their horses. Below a curse rose as a third man stumbled in the darkness almost at the base of the rock.

'Hurry!' Cordell whispered. He heard the man who'd been on the ledge coming more quickly now. Cordell thought he wasn't more than a dozen feet away.

Lebow reached out to grasp the rope. His foot slipped, sending a chunk of ice cascading down the rock. The man below cried out in surprise.

Cordell caught Lebow's arm, holding him back. He pointed downward—at a white face, at starlight touching the cold metal of a gun aimed up at them.

XV

Lebow's breathing was gusty and frightened as Cordell forced him down flat on the rock. 'Keep a hand on the rope,' Cordell ordered. 'As soon as you feel it go slack, start down. Don't wait!'

Lebow's answer was lost in the loud scrape of Cordell's boots over rock. Cordell caught the rope and swung himself up and out with a kick of his legs. The man below shouted and fired. The bullet hit ice, spattering hard shards against Cordell's face. He looked down, saw the white face directly below him. He opened his hands, letting loose of the rope.

Icy air rushed by him. He heard the jarring roar of a handgun, felt the whip of the bullet rip his trousers. Then his feet struck the man, driving him to the ground, absorbing some of the shock of the long fall.

Cordell stumbled and fell. He rolled to his knees, twisting about to find Heddon's man. He lay motionless and crumpled. Cordell staggered to his feet and ran forward, searching for the man's gun. He found it half buried in a thin patch of snow.

He heard Lebow cry out. He picked up the gun and stepped back, looking upward. Lebow was swinging wildly on the rope, his feet fighting for purchase against the rock. The face of the man who'd been on the ledge appeared above Lebow, his gun arm stretched out as he took aim.

Cordell lifted the gun he'd found. He prayed that the barrel wasn't snow clogged. He swung his arm up and fired in one quick motion. His bullet drove past Lebow and thudded into flesh. The man on top of the rock gave a single strangled cry and disappeared.

Now shouting came from the direction of the camp. Hoofs thudded on frozen ground as Heddon's voice roared up. 'Runt? Slim? What the devil's going on?'

Lebow dropped off the rope and landed in a heap beside Cordell. Cordell helped him up. 'Come on,' he said. 'They'll be here in a minute.'

'Where can we go?' Lebow demanded. 'Where is there to go?'

Cordell shook his shoulder roughly. 'After Slim and Runt's horses. If Heddon gets to the cut first, we'll never get out of here alive.'

Cordell pushed Lebow toward the camp, staying close to the wall of rock. Not a dozen feet away, Heddon was shouting as he led his two men through the brush and timber. Cordell held his gun ready in case Heddon or one of his men should stumble onto them. But the three crashed by on the left.

Lebow and Cordell stumbled out of the trees and into the camp. Two horses stood well

137

away from the fire, shifting nervously. Lebow ran to the nearest animal and scrambled to its back. He pulled a rifle excitedly from the saddle boot.

'Put it back until we're in the open!' Cordell ordered. 'The trees will tear it out of your hand.' He lifted himself into the saddle of the other horse, a heavy black with a big barrel and short, powerful legs.

'Follow me,' he said. 'We'll try to outflank Heddon.'

He started the black straight south, moving slowly through the heavy night under the trees. He heard Heddon to the west, crashing his way blindly, trying to find easier going.

Cordell kept up the slow pace until they reached the border of the meadow. He reined west now, picking up speed through the thinning timber. Lebow kept his mount on the heels of Cordell's black, riding lumpishly and awkwardly but staying tight to the saddle.

The sound of Heddon and his men drew closer and then faded as Cordell worked down into the tongue of timber. Then Heddon found an easier route. The hammering of hoofs was sharp and clear.

Cordell drove the black out of the trees and into the open, following the pattern of broken snow left by the pack-train. The moon had risen, throwing down a harsh, revealing light.

Lebow cried suddenly, 'He's getting away. Lansford's getting away from me!'

Cordell lifted his head. The pack-train had reached the cut. Lansford, at the rear, kept up an intermittent fire directed at the lone rider still in the meadow. He sat his horse well out of range of Lansford's gun. Not far from him a huddled figure made a dark blotch against the moonlit snow.

Blanton stepped back to the lead horse long enough to put his rifle in its saddle boot. Then he drove his heavy body forward, slamming it into the wind-drifted snow choking the mouth of the cut. His momentum broke and he backed away, clawing snow from his eyes and beard. He plunged forward again and this time he disappeared.

He came back quickly, caught the reins of the lead horse, and led the pack-train into the cut. Lansford stayed behind Maudie, his rifle ready in case Heddon's man should move into range. But he stayed where he was, slumped on his tired horse.

Cordell watched somberly as the buckskin and then Maudie moved out of sight. By delaying Heddon he had won a partial victory, but as Lansford strode into the cut, Cordell knew he was watching the destruction of eight years of his life.

*　　*　　*

As Lansford disappeared into the cut, Pike Heddon and his two men burst from the trees.

Heddon's deep voice filled the cold air: 'There they are! Pete, head 'em off!'

The man south of the cut was already forcing his weary horse forward. He lifted his rifle now and sent a shot toward Cordell and Lebow. The bullet went wildly into the night.

Heddon cried, 'Tom, Art, spread out! Don't let 'em get back in the trees.'

Cordell twisted around. Heddon's men were wide apart, pushing their horses through unbroken snow. Heddon himself rode directly behind Cordell and Lebow, following the path cut by the pack-train, moving more swiftly. He lifted his rifle and fired.

Lebow cried out in terror as his horse reared up and then fell, blood gushing from a bullet wound in its flank. Cordell turned the black and pulled Lebow up behind the saddle. Bullets thudded viciously into the snow as Cordell swung the black and headed for the cut again.

'The rifle!' Lebow cried. 'I lost my rifle!'

Cordell pulled the rifle out of the black's saddle boot and thrust it at Lebow. 'Aim for Heddon,' he said. He kicked the black into a weaving run.

Ahead, Pete had his horse through the last of the deep drifts between him and the cut. Cordell pulled the handgun from his belt and sent two quick shots at Pete. A third shot struck the rock above the cut, spattering razor sharp shards through the air. Pete howled and threw one hand over his eyes. Cordell triggered his gun again. The hammer clicked harmlessly on an empty casing.

He cast a quick glance behind. Lebow was firing the rifle awkwardly but steadily, forcing Heddon to slow down.

One of Heddon's shots struck near the black, sending it into a wild dance. Cordell swung in the saddle. Pete had dropped his hand from his face. He was so close Cordell could see the blood streaming into his eyes from a cut on his forehead. He had raised his rifle and fired blindly.

Cordell drove the black forward in one final surge. Pete's rifle cracked again as the black struck his horse. Both animals staggered, sending their riders cascading off into the churned snow.

Cordell rolled to his feet. Pete lay limp a dozen feet away. Lebow staggered up, his expression dazed, the rifle still held in his hand. A bullet cut the snow in front of Cordell. Another whined viciously past Lebow's head. Cordell saw that Heddon and his men had stopped riding. All three were taking careful aim.

A bullet scoured across Lebow's hip. He cried out and dashed for the mouth of the cut. The gun slipped out of his hand. He hesitated and then ran on as another bullet whipped near him. He plunged out of the moonlight and into darkness.

Cordell made a sudden run after him. Three rifles slammed their sound at him in chorus. He left his feet in a long dive that carried him to the rifle Lebow had dropped. He hugged it to his chest and rolled into the cut. He scrambled to his feet and plunged forward as a final shot screamed off rock over his head.

Cordell stopped abruptly as the cut made a sharp turn into inky blackness. He looked upward and saw nothing. The stone floor here was bare of snow and smooth to his feet. He realized that this cut was not like the one to the east, but was a natural tunnel through solid rock.

He groped his way forward cautiously, his free hand held in front of him. He stopped to listen. There was no sound but his own breathing.

He called softly, 'Lebow!' Then he heard someone running well ahead of him in the dark. Cordell whispered, 'Lebow! Lansford will be at the other end, waiting for Heddon to come through.'

His voice echoed back at him. The running faded to nothing. Cordell swore. He'd pinned his lone remaining hope of success on Lansford's camping at the far end of the cut because of darkness as well as to guard against Heddon's pursuit. If Lansford was there, the firing in the meadow would have him on the alert. But Cordell still hoped a surprise attack might catch Lansford off guard.

Now, unless he could stop Lebow from charging crazily out of the tunnel, all advantage of surprise would be gone, and Cordell would be pinned down by Heddon at one end of the cut and Lansford and Blanton at the other.

Cordell heard a new sound. Soft murmuring came from behind him. He cocked his head, listening, and then he padded softly back the way he'd come. He reached the sharp turn and stopped. He could make out voices now, and he recognized Pike Heddon's distinctive rumble.

Heddon was saying, 'Keep down and quiet. Shoot at anything that moves.'

Cordell lifted the rifle and stepped around the corner. Moonlight outlined the end of the cut. The forms of three men were barely visible as dark blotches on the stone floor. A fourth man stood back in the meadow, bent over as if he was injured.

Cordell said sharply, 'That's far enough, Heddon.'

Gunfire spattered the darkness. A high bullet struck rock as Cordell dropped to his knees. He fired the rifle twice and went flat to his belly.

Someone cried out in pain. The thick body of Pike Heddon reared up. He ran forward, his gun crashing aimlessly, and then he plunged down on his face.

A man shouted, 'He got the boss! He

got Pike!'

His voice was drowned by a strange cracking sound quivering above the echoes of Heddon's firing. A fist-sized chunk of rock plummeted down from above and crashed a few inches in front of Cordell. He twisted to his feet and ran around the corner, back into the inky darkness. The deep boom of a handgun followed him. The cracking sound became a rumble. Through it he heard a shout of terror, 'The roof's coming down!'

Another rock fell, striking Cordell's shoulder. He plunged on. He hit a wall of stone as the tunnel made another sharp turn. His momentum caromed him around the corner. He stopped abruptly as he saw a faint flicker of firelight reflected off a shallow bend ahead.

The deep rumbling sound turned to a roar as that part of the tunnel roof closer to the meadow collapsed. Cordell stared upward. A crack appeared above his head, widened, and then stopped. The floor and walls around him quivered. The roar of crashing rock began to fade and the dry smell of dust filled the air.

Cordell coughed. He went to his knees, seeking fresher air closer to the floor. He crawled toward the flickering light, guessing that Lansford and Blanton would be waiting, wondering if anyone had lived to come out of the tunnel.

Cordell reached the bend and felt faint

warmth reflected off the rocks. He bellied down and slid cautiously forward until he could see ahead. Momentary relief flooded him as he saw Lebow a few feet away, his hands holding a heavy rock over his head. Lebow let his arms down slowly. 'What was all that noise?' he demanded.

Cordell got to his feet. 'I killed Heddon. Our shots brought the roof of the tunnel down. You and I couldn't go back now if we wanted to.'

He looked past Lebow. The tunnel went on for another twenty feet. A campfire blazed a short distance from its mouth, placed so its light illumined the tunnel's end. Behind the campfire, Cordell made out the tops of trees silvered by the moon.

Lebow said, 'I looked. They're waiting out there. The fire's a trap. They're at another one off to the right, eating venison and sucking up heat—and never taking their eyes off the tunnel.'

His expression changed as concern flickered across it. 'I didn't see the girl nowhere, but I heard them talking. I think they got her back in the woods where it's cold. Blanton said something about her telling where the trail to Mexico was when she got cold enough and hungry enough.' A wild light flared into his eyes as he spoke of Maudie.

Cordell said quickly, 'They won't hurt her as long as they need her.' Lebow nodded and

Cordell added, 'What did Lansford and Blanton do when they heard the noise?'

'Nothing,' Lebow said. 'Blanton wanted to take a look but Lansford wouldn't let him. He said they'd lose their advantage if they didn't stay where they were.'

Cordell nodded grimly. 'The advantage is all theirs.' He started forward. 'Our one chance is to see if there's any way to surprise them.'

'There isn't,' Lebow said. 'They . . .'

He broke off as a high, thin cry echoed from the camp into the tunnel. Wildness gleamed in his eyes.

'The girl! They're hurting her!'

Cordell started forward. Lebow moved with startling quickness, pushing Cordell off balance with one hand and jerking the rifle away with the other. He crashed wildly on past Cordell.

Cordell had been driven back against the wall of the tunnel by Lebow's mad charge. His breath left him. He fought for air. He recovered and ran alter Lebow.

Lebow's charge carried him out of the cut, straight through the fire. His feet scattered burning embers. Cordell swore helplessly as he followed.

He plunged into the open. He had a quick glimpse of the camp. Lansford was on his feet by a small fire, holding a piece of meat in one hand and reaching for his gun with the other. Maudie was on a log well back from the fire, her feet and wrists tied, her face white and pinched from cold and hunger and fear. Blanton stood over her, a knifeblade held to the white skin of her throat.

Lebow's crazed run brought Blanton swinging around, reaching for the gun at his belt. He cleared leather and fired before Lebow's clumsy hands could bring the rifle to bear on him.

Lebow stumbled and went down, the rifle sliding away from him. 'Lebow, by God!' Blanton cried in surprise.

Lansford's gun was on Cordell. 'Lebow—and Cordell too,' he said. His voice was heavy with satisfaction.

XVI

Without breaking stride, Cordell reached down and caught up a length of burning firewood with his bare hand. He threw it underhand as Lansford's gun went off. Lansford was throwing up an arm to protect his face and the bullet kicked into the fire to one side of Cordell.

Maudie cried suddenly, 'Watch out!'

Cordell had a swift glimpse of Blanton as he stepped over Maudie to get enough to one side of Lansford for a clear shot. She rolled, throwing her bound legs frantically against Blanton's heavy ankles. He cursed as he staggered off balance. Righting himself, he lifted a hand to strike at Maudie.

Lebow screamed like a hurt animal and clawed himself out of the dirt. He lurched toward Blanton and caught his arm before it could reach Maudie.

Cordell saw Lansford level his gun for a second shot. He dove, sending his shoulder into Lansford's thighs, driving Lansford over on his back. His gun whipped from his hand and clanged loudly against a rock.

Lansford reached up and hit Cordell viciously in the face. Cordell caught his wrist and jerked, throwing Lansford belly down. He turned and caught both of Lansford's arms to draw them up behind his back. His immediate thought was one of triumph—that Lansford was finally his prisoner.

Lebow's crazed scream rose again, lifting Cordell's head. Lebow had a tight grip on Blanton's arm, and Blanton was throwing Lebow around violently in an effort to shake the thick body loose. Lebow lost his grip and fell heavily to the ground. His fingers scrabbled frantically in the dirt and closed over the hilt of the knife Blanton had dropped when Cordell first appeared. Blanton lifted his gun almost contemptuously and aimed it at Lebow's head.

Lebow surged to his knees, the knife held in both hands. He thrust forward and upward as Blanton fired full into his face. The bullet slammed Lebow backward just as he buried the knife to the hilt at Blanton's beltline. Blanton dropped his gun, stared uncomprehendingly at the knife, took one short step forward, and fell on top of Lebow's still body.

Maudie cried out and turned her head aside as if she wanted to be sick.

Lansford gave a violent jerk that pulled his arms out of Cordell's grip. He leaped to his feet, reaching for the gun he had dropped.

Cordell threw himself full length on the ground, his fingers reaching for the rifle Lebow had lost. He pulled it to him and twisted around onto his knees. Lansford had the gun aimed at him but he was staring down at it, his face white with horror.

Cordell could see the shattered mechanism of the gun. It had broken when Lansford let it fly from his hand against the rock. Cordell lifted the rifle slowly.

'Throw it away, Lansford.'

Lansford took a step backward, toward the fire burning in front of the cut. 'You won't kill me,' he said mockingly. 'You want me alive too badly.'

'I won't kill you,' Cordell agreed, 'but I won't worry if I shatter both your legs.' He lifted the gun slightly. 'You have five seconds to get over here.'

Lansford cried mockingly, 'Come and get me!' He threw the useless gun at Cordell and leaped backward over the fire. He turned in the air like a cat and landed facing the cut. Without losing momentum, he dashed into the tunnel and out of sight.

Cordell drove a shot at Lansford's legs, but the bright firelight half blinded him and he missed. He let the rifle dip as Lansford ran into the tunnel, his footsteps echoing loudly and then fading into silence.

Cordell rose and walked toward Maudie, stopping to pick a knife out of the litter of camp gear. He knelt by her and sawed the ropes from her wrists and ankles.

'You're all right?'

'I will be once I get warm and have

150

something to eat,' she said. She grimaced as she flexed her fingers, stiff from her wrists having been tied so long.

She looked carefully at Cordell. 'Mont . . . ?' she asked.

Cordell stood up. 'I'm going after him,' he told her. He handed her the rifle. 'If he comes out first, don't wait. Shoot.'

She thrust the rifle back at him. 'Take it, please. He has a belt knife.'

Cordell said, 'I know.' He walked to the fire and selected a piece of pitchpine burning only on one end. 'I want Lansford alive,' he explained. 'If I take a weapon, I'll be tempted to kill him.'

He strode to the tunnel and then moved more slowly to the first bend. He stopped here and called softly, 'The tunnel's blocked, Lansford. There's no place for you to go.'

Lansford answered mockingly out of distant darkness, his voice more of an echo than direct sound: 'I told you before—come and get me.'

Cordell held his make-shift torch high and stepped around the bend. The feeble light was swallowed by blackness three feet from its source. Cordell walked forward warily, keeping the torch high, his eyes straining for some sign of movement. Dust still hung in the still air, thickening as he went deeper into the tunnel. It stung his eyes and clogged his nostrils. He fought a desire to find fresher air close to the floor and plodded doggedly on.

He reached the sharp corner in the middle of the tunnel and paused. A faint sound as of rock scraping rock reached him. He stepped swiftly around the corner, holding the torch up and away from himself. It was barely burning now in the foul, dust-laden air.

But there was light enough for Cordell to see the cold gleam reflected from Lansford's eyes, to make out the form of his body as he crouched on a pile of rubble only a few paces ahead.

Lansford shouted a meaningless sound and came to his feet. A rock spurted from his hand and struck the torch. It spun to the floor and went out, bringing the choking darkness down like a solid wave.

Cordell heard the scrape of Lansford's boots and braced himself for a rush. He went to his knees as he felt the air stir. A rock whizzed over his head. Another came quickly, catching him in the face, ripping flesh from his chin. He went over on his back, momentarily dazed by the shock of pain.

Lansford's feet hammered as he rushed forward. Cordell squeezed himself against the side of the tunnel to keep from being trampled. He threw out an arm, catching Lansford's ankle. He pulled with his full strength.

As Lansford came down on top of Cordell, the probing heat of a knifeblade searched Cordell's ribs, causing him to lose his grip.

Lansford reared up to strike again.

Cordell reached blindly upward. The knifeblade slashed across his knuckles. Then his fingers found a wiry wrist. He closed them down and threw his weight into a sharp backward twist. Lansford screamed as his bone broke with a brittle snap. The knife clattered to the floor of the tunnel.

Cordell dropped Lansford's wrists and twisted his fingers in Lansford's hair. He jerked his arm forward and drove his bloody free hand into Lansford's face, throwing into the blow all of the pent up anger of eight long years. He felt Lansford's mouth give under his knuckles. He struck again, and Lansford went limp.

Pain and exhaustion swept over Cordell. He fell forward, striking his face against Lansford's chest. He pushed himself up with a grunt and crawled to his knees. He turned and reached back, picking up Lansford's ankle. He began a slow, steady crawling through the dusty darkness.

He came into the open air, Lansford bumping soddenly behind him. He crawled around the fires and to the log where Maudie had been tied. She was nowhere in sight.

Cordell dropped Lansford's ankle and got groggily to his feet. He swayed as he peered around. 'Maudie?'

She came out of the darkness under the trees, the rifle in her hand. She stared from

153

Cordell to Lansford. The rifle dropped at her feet and she ran forward with a soft cry.

Cordell held out his arms and clasped emptiness as he pitched forward on his face.

*   *   *

Cordell awakened to daylight and warm sunshine. He ate, helped Maudie bandage the knifewound in his side, and fell asleep. He woke twice, once to make sure that Lansford was still lashed to the tree where Maudie had tied him the night before, and again to eat.

When he opened his eyes again, it was to the brightness of moonlight filtering through the trees. Maudie lay wrapped in her blankets only inches away.

Cordell saw moonlight reflected from her eyes and knew that she was awake. He said, 'Tomorrow we'll walk down Paradise. We can stake the horses here and hide the gold until the snow goes off the meadow and we can bring up the mules.'

Maudie stirred. 'What will you do with Mont?'

'Take him to jail in Tucson.'

'And then?'

'After his trial, I'll go where the Army sends me,' Cordell said.

'I expected you to say that,' she murmured.

'I'm due for a captaincy,' Cordell said slowly. 'I'll able to ask for a post where I can

154

take a wife.'

'I expected you to say that too,' she answered softly.

Cordell's laugh blended with hers as he reached out and drew her to him through the moonlight.